Victoria has been through a lot of hardship, which led to bouts of depression, anxiety, eating disorders, self-hatred, self-harm, and a suicide attempt. At 22, she became a published author of an auto biographical/self-help book, *Trust Me: Through the Eyes of a Survivor*, which talks about it all. Since her role as an author, she has also become a motivational speaker. Now 27, this is her first novel, also based on her life. She is passionate about mental health awareness and support, and she strives to make a difference, help others, and save lives through her experiences and her writing.

Dedicated to my beautiful aunt, Andrea, without whom, I would not be here today.
There are not enough words in the English language to describe my love for you.
Love and miss you every day, my sweet angel.

Andrea Cerone.
June 6, 1968–September 25, 2019.

Victoria Caputo

THE STORYTELLER

AUSTIN MACAULEY PUBLISHERS™

LONDON • CAMBRIDGE • NEW YORK • SHARJAH

A CIP catalogue record for this title is available from the British Library.

ISBN 9781528912174 (Paperback)
ISBN 9781528951197 (ePub e-book)

www.austinmacauley.com

First Published 2023
Austin Macauley Publishers Ltd®
1 Canada Square
Canary Wharf
London
E14 5AA

Mom, I am inspired and in awe of your strength every single day. I will never be able to fully describe my gratitude and love for you. So, for everything you've ever done for me, continue to do for me, and for helping me beyond belief to get to this point, I thank you.

Maria, you have pushed me to go beyond my limits and be the best version of myself I could be. You've shown me strength in weakness, and light in darkness, so for that, I thank you.

Jenn and Joanne, for your constant support, and unwavering belief in me during such tragic times, and for being two of the best faux aunts I could have ever asked for, I thank you.

Table of Contents

Part One
Past

Chapter One
Well-Behaved Women Rarely Make History

Port Chester, New York. God, how I miss it. My house, my friends, even my Catholic school, even though I'm not really religious anymore. I remember this one time, in third grade, I had to pick a famous person to focus a biography project on. I had to learn about and embody this character, even dress like her for the presentation. I chose the "Unsinkable Molly Brown", a survivor of the RMS Titanic travesty in 1912. She sealed her place in history when she helped evacuate the sinking ship, putting others' lives before her own. When finally convinced to get on a lifeboat and save herself, she encouraged the crewmen of lifeboat #6 to turn around and go back to save more lives. As a young girl, her courage and strength always inspired me, and I wanted to be just like her. She did what she wasn't supposed to do and ended up saving lives. So, what if she went against a guy? Well-behaved women rarely make history, and I wanted to be a history maker.

I thought it was easy to be strong, but after my family decided to leave our home and move somewhere totally different that had no place for me, I realised that I was not unsinkable like Molly Brown.

Greenwich, Connecticut. Not really the place for me. I tried to keep an open mind but as a shy, little ten-year-old girl, I had no idea what to expect. The first day of fourth grade was absolutely terrifying, as was almost every day after that. While elementary school was scary, it doesn't even come close to middle school and high school. In seventh grade, some girls thought it would be fun destroy the little bit of social life by spreading some stupid (yet important to immature, high school students) rumours about me. Why? To this day, I really have no idea. I don't think I did anything to them, but I guess they were bored and saw me as an easy target.

Suddenly, I was being picked on, harassed, and tormented on nearly a daily basis. School for me was a dog-eat-dog world, and those dogs chewed me up and spit me out like I was nothing. I was just a scared, lost little puppy, all alone with no one in a world full of big dogs, and I still am. I ask for help; nothing ever gets done. People watch the bullying occur; nothing ever gets done. Nothing except being taken advantage of by your English teacher. I mean. I didn't have any friends, so I turned to him for support and let's just say, that wasn't the kind of comfort I was looking for. Years have gone by and the bullying hasn't changed. The teacher has since been fired, as many girls came forward about what was happening, but that doesn't just make the aftermath of something like that just go away. People still hate me, but honestly, I don't think any of them can hate me as much as I hate myself. So here I am now: a lonely, depressed senior in this dog pound you call high school who has no one but herself. Well, herself and her journal.

When you look in the mirror, what do you see? You see your face, your body, and your legs looking back at you; that's the normal reflection. I am not normal. I look into the mirror, and I see two people. First, I see a warrior. Her stance is so strong and her power reflects onto me through the sparkling glass of the mirror. Her empowerment shines and she is ready to fight. She is ready to do what she needs to do to survive. As quickly as she comes, she fades slowly out of my line of vision. The figure morphs into a frail, weak woman. Her sad eyes stare into my soul and I can feel her tears on my cheeks. This time, it's different; this presence is frighteningly sad. She is ready to give up; she is sick of fighting. Her scars show that she's been fighting for a while. In the blink of an eye, she disappears as well, and I'm left there alone. These women are my reflection. I may not be normal, but these two women, they are me.

Would my life have taken this turn if I stayed in Port Chester? I really don't know. I know my parents have always done whatever they did to give me a better life, so I'd never blame any of this on them. They've loved me my whole life, even with all the bullshit I've put them through. They're amazing, and honestly, they deserve a better daughter than me. Still, I can't help but wonder how my life would be different if we never moved. It doesn't matter, obviously, what's done is done.

Regardless, I am who I am, even if it's someone, or two people, that I despise.

Chapter Two
Just Me and My Journal

I've always been a very shy, private person. Someone who has always kept her deep, inner thoughts and feelings to herself. Writing has always been both an outlet and a hobby of mine. Whenever I'm lonely and have no one to talk to, which is about ninety nine percent of the time, my journal has always been there for me.

It really helps me to write down the sick, twisted, depressing things I think and feel. First of all, I have no one to tell them too, but also, why would I burden someone with the horrific, dark things that go on in my messed-up head? That's not all I write though. I find comfort in creating stories and characters outside of myself. As someone with such low self-esteem and such a deep self-hatred, sometimes it's nice to pretend that I'm someone else doing something amazing. Like a beautiful actress filming a moving somewhere international, ideally Italy or Spain. Or a successful businesswoman married to the man of her dreams. Or literally anyone else other than myself, living any other life other than mine.

I find it nice to create and write stories that may seem somewhat random. Focusing on a different setting, persona or life other than just my own. It gives me hope knowing that there could be someone out there living the dream that I am writing about and so desperately want, even if it's not me. My dream of being loved, happy and experiencing the beauty and adventure of the world rather just being stuck in the dark depths of this society. Good for that person, whoever they may be.

Another dream of mine has always been to become a published author someday. Not self-published, but actually discovered by a publishing agency. Finding someone who believes in my skills and power of writing just as much as I do. F. Scott Fitzgerald once said "You don't write because you want to say something, but rather, you write because you have something to say." and boy, do I have a lot to say.

I think about what it would be like to be a published author with her own book. It's crazy to me that people would be reading my writing at any given point of any given day. I could be sitting on the couch watching television and I would have no idea that at that exact moment, someone could be reading a book that I wrote. Reading words that I put together myself into a sentence. I would have no idea that at that exact moment, someone could be buying my book. Finding it worthy of their time and money. Just thinking about it is surreal.

The English language can be so impactful, more than most people think. That's why so many abusers and bullies out there fight verbally. They know that mental abuse can be way more damaging to someone than physical abuse. They know how impactful what they say can be and some of them even think they aren't doing anything wrong because "words are just words". Sticks and stones may break my bones but words will never hurt me? Bullshit.

I believe in the power of words, and while people misuse that power, I want to bring that power out in a positive way. I believe that words can change the world, and I want to change the world.

The best part about the whole thing is that words last forever. It doesn't really matter how long I make it on this Earth as long as I put my thoughts and feelings to paper first. In my situation, that's a blessing because honestly, who knows what's going to happen. I'm more of a "do what I say, not what I do" kind of person. I've always been good at giving advice but not so good at taking my own advice. I have a story, one that could be told for generations after I'm gone. One that people need to hear so that the world doesn't let down anyone like it has me. It's too late for me, I know that, I've accepted that, but it's not too late for others struggling like I have.

After what this world and its inhabitants have done to me, my story deserves to be heard dammit. It's a relief to know though that I may be completely messed up mentally, but I can still impact the world in a positive way if I was to ever become a published author. That's the dream, and one that I'm damn proud of.

Chapter Three
Calling You Home

Fifteen years ago, and yet I recall the emotions and thoughts like it was yesterday. He looked so fragile, like if I touched him, he would break. His eyes were closed and yet I tried so hard to stare into them. He gripped my hand as tightly as his strength would allow. To me, it felt like nothing, but to him, it was everything. He slowly opened his eyes and fixated his weak vision on my innocent face. Feeling his stare, I met his gaze, and he smiled. I haven't seen him smile in so long, I almost forgot what it looked like. I knew he was scared, but I knew his smile was sincere.

After choking back my cries for so long, a tear finally let go. He noticed it, and with all his might, he lifted his hand, and wiped the one lonely tear that ran down my cheek. I recognised his touch and felt the coldness of his golden bracelet; I've rarely ever seen him without it on. Graciously and carefully, he used his left hand to slide the bracelet off of his right wrist. I let out another tear and his frail hand grazed my cheek again. He took my hand, and slowly, but perfectly, slid the bracelet onto my wrist. As I released a third tear, he kissed my hand and placed it onto his chest. In that moment, I knew what was going on. My nine-year-old self finally understood that within the next few hours, I would no longer have my grandfather.

Losing a loved one at a young age like that was very confusing for me. It took me a while to realise what was actually going on. It took me years to fully understand why I lost him. Why my grandmother lost her husband. Why my mother and aunt lost their dad. Why my sister and I lost our grandfather. I mean I knew he was sick but I'm talking about the worldly, philosophical reasons as to why we lost someone so incredible who we loved so dearly. I'm not really religious, but I'd like to think Heaven exists. God calls the best people home when he needs them, and my Pop was definitely the best.

When my Pop died, it was the first time I've ever seen my father cry. I was only nine years old but I felt like that I had to be strong for my family. I wanted to be there for them and I didn't want them to know how devastated I truly was. They had enough to worry about, and I didn't want to be another concern. So, I did the best I could to put on a tough face for them even though on the inside my heart was complete shattered.

My poor grandmother. My poor mother and aunt. What they must have been going through, I can't imagine. I lost someone very close to me too, but I can't imagine losing a husband or a father, especially when he was only sixty-four years old. He still had so much life left to live and so many more memories to make here with us. They needed me to be there for them, and I was; that is, until they needed me the most. I was so young and so afraid to share my emotions regarding everything with the fear that I would make things worse on everyone, so I decided not to go to my Pop's funeral.

I knew how hard it was going to be for me to control myself. All of those people, all of those flowers, all of those tears. I would have lost it. Instead of going to the funeral I went to school and acted like it was just another day. People must have thought I was heartless. I wasn't there for my family or for my Pop that day. To this day, not going to his funeral is one of my utmost biggest regrets.

When I start to think about that and how I let everyone down that day, I try to take myself to a good memory with my Pop. One of the many vacations we used to take as a family. A birthday; we used to celebrate them all of course no matter how old you were turning, and he always made it feel special. Usually when I think about my Pop, though, I think about his chair. That old, brown rocking chair. God how I loved that thing. You can hear it creek from a mile away. He sat in that chair every chance he could, usually listening to the voice of Alex Trebek, immediately followed by some idiot thinking that he or she is correct. They weren't, ever. He always was though. He always told me that he'd get on that show someday. "I could do this, and I could win a whole bunch of money for the family." That's what he'd say to me as I sat on his lap, not watching the show and the idiots it displayed, but feeling his warmth surround me. These moments are engraved in my mind; so long ago, and yet, I remember it all. I remember all the voices around me circling my head. I remember his arms enveloping me oh so tightly. What I remember most? That old brown rocking chair. That is clear as day.

I still wonder if my Pop is disappointed in me for not going to his funeral. At this point though, he definitely has a lot more to be disappointed in me for.

Chapter Four
A Blog for the
Lonely and Heartbroken

"How do you expect me to love with a broken heart?
How do you expect me to breathe without air?
You were my heart.
You were my oxygen.
You were my everything.
And now I'm nothing.
How can you expect me to go on being nothing?
I can't. And I don't want to be alone."

A lot of my writing has been about you lately. My journal has become some kind of compilation of blogs posts for the lonely and heartbroken. Love is such a complicated thing, but being in love is a whole different story. And when you're in love; true, genuine, love, and you get your heart broken? Geez. It's rough. The mix of emotions is such a roller coaster, and on top of the many mental illnesses that I have been plagued with, I won't lie, it's been a killer. How am I supposed to accept the fact that you chose her over me?

"You've promised me countless times that things would be different for us

But today you proved to me that everything is exactly the same and it always will be You made it very clear that I am not and never will be your first choice. With every tremor my body was shaking you off of me like a fly that just won't quit. With every vomit my core was releasing you out of its soul to escape your manipulative charm. At the end of the day, you are always going to pick her over me and where does that leave me?

Even before I stood in the shadows all by myself while I watch you with her. Me on the sidelines.

You played me like a two-bit fiddle and watched as I cracked under the pressure of the music.

My words were cheapened. You told me that you cared about me when really you only cared about yourself.

How am I supposed to accept a plastic apology that you made so many times before but then failed to keep?

How can someone be the best thing that has ever happened to me while also being the one who ruined me?

You took my heart and mangled it like a lion hunting her prey and killing it in the jungle.

So let it be known that she fought with the strength of a Trojan, but alas, her love was her Achilles Heel."

The nights are the hardest, and that's when I get most of my writing done, especially about my broken heart. When I can't sleep because I'm thinking of you. I close my eyes and I see you. I empty my mind and yet I still think of you. Isn't that the way love should be? I've tried so hard to keep myself grounded that I've actually fallen, harder than I ever have before. And no matter how much I feel like I should get up and continue walking, I just lay there in awe of these emotions that I never thought possible in my life. And when I do try to get up, I just can't.

I can't do anything anymore. I can't think straight because I can't stop thinking about you, wondering what you're doing and picturing you and her together. I can't sleep because all I do is cry. I can't eat because I am always so sick to my stomach all of the time. I can't stop crying because you've broken my heart in a way no one else ever could. I can't stop hating myself for letting my guard down, opening up to you and believing your lies. I can't stop thinking of what you've done to me.

"I pictured everything.

I pictured the wedding we'd have. Our family and friends coming together to celebrate the official joining of two soulmates. Maybe you'd cry, maybe you wouldn't, but I would be so overwhelmed by the fact that my dream for so long was finally coming true that I would be crying. I'd be in a white dress, of course. Probably not as traditional as most brides, but that's okay. You'd look so handsome, as you always do, in your tux. My father would walk me down the aisle and hold my hand even tighter when it feels it trembling from all of the mixed emotions in my head. He'd pass me off to you, shake your hand, and I'd be standing there with you, ready for the beginning of the rest of our lives.

I pictured the house we would have. The traditional, white picket fence that everyone talks about. Yeah, we'd have that. It would border our two-story house that would immediately become our home. You would come home at the end of your long day as one of the CEOs of some huge company. I would already be home to greet you since I would work from home most of the time as an author and mental health advocate. Dinner would be ready, and we'd spend the night together, watching our favourite television shows and talking about our day.

I pictured the family we would have. I saw our first-born son being named after you. I love your name. It's unique and elegant in the most beautiful way. Every big brother needs a little sister to look out for and protect, so I also saw a little girl in our future. I was thinking that we'd possibly name her after your mom; I think she'd like that. Both of us being animal lovers, we would of course get a pet. I was thinking a puppy and a kitten that would grow up together. They would have such a unique friendship, just like we did when we first became close. And we'd come up with their names together. The kitten would sit on the top of the couch and look outside as the puppy would play with the kids outside in the backyard that was surrounded by that traditional white picket fence that we'd have.

I pictured everything, not knowing that you were too picturing the same thing I was, just with someone other than me."

This wasn't the plan. It wasn't supposed to end like this. We had our whole lives ahead of us. Together forever, right? Not so much anymore. I saw the way she looked at you, and I saw the way you looked at her. Your eyes met as if each of you had found the greatest treasure of all. It was like when you and I first laid eyes on each other; I can spot that look from a mile away. Your loins quivered for her like they used to for me. Your body ached in sight of her, as if you hoped she would take you right there and then. I'm not as stupid as you may think. I remember when my presence would bring a smile to your face; now I just see an expression of un-interest and boredom. In your defence, you're not the only one who's gotten sick of me. But in my defence, a girl can dream, right? You're not the only one who's ever left. Of course, you left me; who in their right mind would stay? Maybe that's the way my life is supposed to be. Maybe that's what I deserve. The memories will always linger in the back of my mind, but I can't honestly say I wasn't expecting anything less. Sometimes I wonder if maybe this actually was your plan all along.

"He loves me. He loves me not. He loves me. He loves me not. Well? Which one is it?

He loves me.

We were lying in bed the other night, both with a nice buzz, and he couldn't keep his hands off of me. He caressed my cheek with the softest touch as a tear rolled down his face and he whispered: "God, you're beautiful. Every single curve and shape of you is perfect. God definitely spent some extra time on you." I blushed, as I always did when he complimented me. Even though I didn't see what he saw in me, it felt so good that someone like him could see some type of beauty within me. I've never been loved like this before. It was amazing.

He loves me not.

Little did I know, it was all a lie. Just useless banter to keep me coming back until he found someone better. He had someone else he truly loved, and love more than me. Tears running and arms bleeding, he knew we never had a chance, but he kept stringing me along for the ride, and I was too blinded by love to notice. Everything felt so real to me; how could I have been so stupid? I guess I can't blame him for not loving me, but I can blame him for messing with and breathing my heart. My heart is shattered beyond repair and my mind is completely destroyed. I remember every single thing you've ever said to me, yet I can't ever remember to forget you.

He loves me. He loves me not. He loves me. He loves me not. Somehow, I still don't know..."

Do you remember me? We used to stand in the sun and dance in the rain. Then one day she came along and I guess you just forgot. But I'll never forget. You were my everything. You were my sun, and my rain. And now I'm left all alone, stuck in the shadows and thunderstorms all by myself.

I don't know how to explain to you what I'm going through, because you'll never know, but try to think about this. My whole life, I have been loved in the wrong way. Abused in every sense of the word by countless people, especially men. I never thought I would ever be loved in the right way in my entire life. You did though. You loved me in the most perfect way. Whether it was real or not, regardless, you loved me in the most amazing, magical way. It felt unreal, like I was in a fairy-tale. And then one day, it's just gone. I was given a glimpse of it, a tease, just to have it taken away from me. And what it's doing to me, I can't even explain. I'm not one who's speechless often, but when it comes to this, what I'm feeling and thinking and going through, words cannot describe.

I feel so lost in this world. Sometimes I find myself still lying-in bed, feeling for your heartbeat and searching for your scent. I've always said you were my home, and now I'm homeless. I cut my arms and thighs with sharp objects, and yet, this hurts more. No bullet could ever destroy my heart like you have.

How do people get over such tremendous heartbreak? Not only have I never been in love before I met you, but I never thought I even had a soulmate out there. I was okay with being on my own, I really was, that is, when I thought that's what was destined for me. Now that I know you exist, I'm not okay with it. You were created for me, and I was created for you. But you don't love me or want me like I love and want you. How does that make sense? It doesn't; we are meant to be together. I would treat you so right, and make you the happiest man alive. I know it, and that's coming from someone who hates herself. If there is one thing, I am happy with about myself, it's that I give my all and everything into the people I love. My whole life has been a struggle, and I really thought that this was finally my time for some happiness. Little did I know, you were just using me until someone better came along. Even so, nothing will change the fact that I know we are meant to be together. Not everyone's lucky enough to meet their soulmate. And now I have to pretend like I never found mine.

Chapter Five
Just Me and My Journal...
and My Razor

I've always been a quiet person. I've always kept to myself and always "felt too much", whatever that means. Things hit me hard, yes, and I am a sensitive person, yes, I would never deny that. I'm always sad, and I'm always feeling like I'm on the verge of crying. I feel like I am always just drowning in a pool of sadness and suffocating under the weight of depression, and everyone around me is breathing fine and just watching me from above. As I got older, I really began to understand why people smoke until their lungs turn black, or why they drink until their liver shuts down, or why they throw themselves off buildings. Being a human in this life is tough, and it's even tougher for a clinically depressed, self-loathing teenage girl.

I can never turn my brain off to stop thinking about all of the hardships I have gone in my life and how miserable I now am today. I can never feel anything but sadness or emptiness. I need a break from the mental anguish. The only thing I have found that somewhat works, even if for just a few minutes, is turning that mental pain into a pain that I can handle better: physical.

Self-harm. What a complicated concept to wrap your head around. Trying to fathom how a person can willingly hurt him or herself, it's impossible. Well, that is until you indulge in the destructive habit yourself.

The first time I hurt myself, I honestly had no idea what I was doing. What do I use? How far was far enough? Most importantly, was it going to help? Self-harm was something I heard about and read about but never did I think I would get to the point of trying it. I was desperate though, and willing to try anything to subside the emotional and mental pain.

I tried a bunch of methods, but the most common technique, cutting, stuck with me. Dragging the blade across my skin, feeling the pain, seeing the blood drip out of my skin. God, what a rush. My fear was what would happen when the pain and rush of cutting was no longer enough. What was the next step? Was there one in between self-harm and suicide? I have no idea, but I figured I'd worry about crossing that bridge when I got to it.

Trust me, I don't endorse this kind of behaviour, but whatever gets me through each day alive, right? Who would have thought that this one-time, desperate, destructive mode of survival would become my only way to survive? So much for a one time, emergency coping mechanism.

Now it's over five years later and it's become a regular, everyday occurrence.

A necessity I need at least three to four times a day. It's an addiction, really. The way a smoker craves nicotine and a drinker craves alcohol, I crave the pain. I need the pain, and now I'm stuck. Stuck in a continuous, bloody loop that spirals more and more out of control every single day. Every time I encounter an asshole at school, every time I get a bad grade, every time I look in the mirror, I'm driven to the comfort of my razor. After living like this for so long, I can't imagine living any other way. Don't get me wrong, I wish I never picked up that razor for the first time that day. On the other hand, if I never did, would I still be alive today? I really do not know.

The craziest part about all of this? It took about four years for anyone to really notice (or care, maybe) that something was wrong. There was one time in math class that my sleeve inched up my arm a little bit when reaching out to take a paper from my teacher. My scarred wrist was exposed just enough for her to see. She looked at my wrist, then up at me. Her eyes met mine and I just stood there, frozen in fear. Was she going to pull me out of class and yell at me? Was she going to tell someone? My mind raced, expecting the worst from her. Instead, she just stared at me and shook her head with a look of disgust like I've never seen. She mumbled quietly, "Just go back to your seat, Tori." That's it. It was never talked about or brought up again. No help was offered. No support, no guidance, nothing. It was in that moment that I realised that nobody really cared and to most people, ignorance really was bliss.

The truth is nobody ever really knows how much anyone else is truly hurting or suffering. You could be standing right next to someone who is completely broken and shattered on the inside and you would not even know anything was wrong. It's scary, really. The harder truth is that when someone does know that a person is truly suffering, they can ignore it so easily like my math teacher did that day.

Since that incident, I stopped caring as much too. Of course, I still hid the scars behind the Band-Aids and the long-sleeved shirts, but I definitely did not go out of my way anymore. Sadly, but not surprisingly, nobody continued to notice and my theory stood corrected. Nobody noticed, and if they did, they didn't care. I was wrong: it's not just me and my journal. It's me, my journal, and my razors too.

Chapter Six
Rooftop Access

Is suicide a selfish act? I guess it can be seen as one. You leave the people who love you with sadness, anger, and possibly even guilt. You put people through pain and probably leave them with many, lifelong questions that they won't ever get an answer to. Is that selfish? It depends on whom you ask. If you ask someone like me, I'll say no, suicide is not a selfish act. To me, what's selfish is asking someone to continue to live like this. In a life that I can't stand. In a body that I despise. With a brain that I hate. That seems selfish too, don't you think?

I'm not saying suicide is a good act, I would never say that. Nobody deserves to be beaten down by life so much that they feel dying is the best-case scenario.

There are many people out there who feel like suicide is the answer to their problem. I don't condone suicide, I never will, but unfortunately, just because someone doesn't deserve to feel this way doesn't mean that they don't. I am more of a "do what I say and not what I do" kind of person. If someone tells me they are feeling suicidal, I will stay up all night with them to make sure they are okay and that they know there is help and hope out there and that they need to keep living for the people who love them. On the other hand, I am also one of those people who just wants to die and move on from the lifelong, ongoing struggles of my hated, depressing life.

Suicide. A word that scares most people but in a sick way, actually comforts me. Knowing that there is a way out if things ever get really bad to a point where I just can't go on. That can be seen as pathetic, I know that, but if knowing that option exists helps me get through life a little bit better, then so be it. I know how twisted that sounds, but you know what's even worse? A society and a world that leads people to feel that way.

I've had quite a few close calls with suicide. Not quite a few suicide attempts, but quite a few almost suicide attempts. The most recent one happened a few days ago and it was probably that closest call I've had thus far.

I was walking around outside on a rainy day in New York City, listening to my music, feeling the gentle raindrops on my head and just trying to zone out everything and everyone around me. No destination and music drowning out the world around me are the best kinds of walks. I was walking through an alleyway when I came across an unmarked door. I analysed the door and then the building around it, realising that most likely it was some kind of a warehouse that nobody really uses anymore. I start to push the door open and it lets out a long, loud creaking noise. Clearly that door hasn't been opened in a while. Once inside, I explore my surroundings. Dust, empty beer bottles, more dust, cigarette butts, old cardboard. Boring. I turn around to face the door I came in through and see another door off the side. This door, though, wasn't unmarked. It read "ROOF TOP ACCESS" across the middle. I took my headphones off, put them in my pocket with my phone and slowly reach for the doorknob. Suddenly, I found myself in a situation that almost seemed to perfect to be true. It was like an out of body experience. I was on the outside looking in at this girl who had lost all control.

The heavy door slams behind her. Looking up at the tower of stairs, she begins to climb. With every step, another thought comes to mind. Step. Thought. Step. Thought. With every breath, she thinks of another reason that supports her hypothesis. Breathe. Think. Breathe. Think.

Nothing to listen to but the quiet gentle raindrops and the sound of her footsteps, she finally makes it to the top of the building. On the rooftop, she stands, still as a gargoyle. She looks out at the stormy grey sky, feeling the chill of the wind brush up against her body. She lifts her head, letting the raindrops fall where they may. Her mind begins to wander again.

"Will this be it?

Has the moment finally come? Can I go through with it?

I have no other choice."

All of the sudden, the storm begins and the once quiet, gentle raindrops start to fall harder. The roar of thunder and the pierce of lightning interrupt her thoughts. Slowly, but ready, she approaches the ledge before her. She looks down and the buildings look like bugs. The cars look like specks on the ground and the pedestrians look like nothing. One more step, and she could just fall off the face of the Earth into an ignorant bliss.

"Yes.

No. Yes. No.

What do I do?"

Her mind raced back and forth as quickly as the lighting struck around her. "Don't do it.

Do it. Stop.

Just jump already!"

She began to fathom what was about to happen. One step forward, and she'd be gone. One step backward, and she'd still be here. This one simple step would change her entire life.

All of the sudden, I snapped back into reality and before I knew it, I was back in my body on the ledge of this seemingly abandoned building.

Turns out I was right; it was too perfect to be true. I took a long, deep breath and stepped back off the ledge. I collapsed to the floor of the rooftop as tears filled my eyes. I sat in the corner of that rooftop shaking for what seemed like forever before I found the physical and mental strength in myself to get up and start making my way down the stairs back to ground level. Was it fear that stopped me? I'm not sure. Was this going to be the last time I tried to end it all? I knew it wouldn't be.

Chapter Seven
Farewell to My Eight Heartbeats

That night I got home and went straight to my bed. I've always had a hard time sleeping but my bed comforted me regardless. Being wrapped up in my comforter so nothing and no one could get to me was always a happy place for me. I got in bed and just laid there, trying to wrap my head around the whole situation that just occurred, both inside and outside of myself. The pain and agony that led me to this point was still there. The reasons and feelings that made me want to die still existed. The desire of wanting to be gone and stop the suffering still burned inside of me. So why didn't I jump?

Could it have been too impulsive? Or too sloppy? If I'm going to do this, it needs to be done right. If I'm going to put my family through this, they need to know that it was my choice. That I am confident and happy in this decision. That I am okay with this fate.

I unwrap myself from my comforter and jump out of my bed. I walk over to my desk where I fumble through some drawers, looking for a clean sheet of paper and a working pen. How can I make this somewhat bearable? Who do I address it to? Luckily, I've always had a way with words. Alright, here we go:

"Mom and Dad,
I'm sorry..."

Nope, that sucks.

"I just can't do this anymore..."

No, that sounds too harsh. Too blunt, I think.

"Mom and Dad,
This isn't your fault. I'll be happier this way."

No, that sounds just awful and sad.

Every thirty seconds or so I was crumpling up a piece of paper, throwing it in the trash and searching through my desk again for another piece of clean paper.

What do I really want to convey here? Is suicide a selfish act? Not to me. That's an important one. Also, the fact that I really tried to stick it out. I tried, I struggled, but I did do my best. Nobody understands how hard I tried and what I've been through, but that's not their fault. Lastly, that this is a destiny that I have accepted and come to terms with.

I've been looking at this all wrong. I've never been a direct writer. I'm better with metaphors and stuff. Definitely a stronger poet, too. Isosyllabic, eight syllables per line, eight-line stanza? Might as well challenge myself. This could be the most important poem I ever write, not to mention, the last one I ever write.

After about a half hour or so, I got it:

"To whom it may concern:
Pen in hand, she closes her eyes
And reflects on the past events,
Everything that led to this point.
She decides that it is the time.
Her eyes spring open as she writes:
'On her tombstone, she requested
If you haven't known my struggle,
Shame on you for judging my pain.

Farewell to my eight heartbeats.
Love You Always,
Tori

I sat there looking at the note for what seemed like forever. Reading each line, examining each word, over and over and over again. It was perfect. It was a masterpiece. In that moment, I know that I was ready to make the biggest decision of my life. A decision that no human being should ever even have to think about, let alone make, yet unfortunately, I do. I don't know when and I don't know how, but the decision has been made and my mind is made up.

I place the note in my coat pocket and wander back over to my bed. I lay down and stare at my popcorn ceiling. I count the bumps on the ceiling in my head. That tends to put me to sleep. One, two, three, four. My eyes start to drift a little.

Five, six, seven, eight. I close my eyes and let out a sigh of relief, knowing that soon the pain and suffering would come to an end. I can't remember the last time I went to bed and fell asleep so relaxed.

Chapter Eight
Obscure Destination to Heaven

Weeks have gone by and that note has been in my coat pocket the whole time. I've been waiting for the right moment; the right opportunity. I assumed that when it was the right time, I'd just know it. The more I thought about it though, the more I wondered what I was really waiting for. After years of bullying, cutting, loneliness and self-loathing, that moment and that opportunity should be coming any day now.

I laid in bed questioning myself for what seemed like hours. I needed a break and decided to go for drive. Nobody was home so I knew nobody would ask where I was going, which was a big relief. Driving always gave me time to clear my head. Not having to think about where I'm going, just listening to the music blasting from the radio with the windows rolled all the way down. That always seemed to help take my mind off of things.

There are a lot of back roads where I live. Very secluded, wooded, windy, nearly hidden, roads. I like to drive around back there because there aren't many cars and I enjoy the solitude from nothing and no one around. After about thirty minutes of driving around, nothing was happening. My mind wasn't clearing like it usually does. Frustrated, I pull over onto a narrow, dirt road and the tears just start flowing. Why wasn't this working? One of my only healthy coping mechanisms doesn't work anymore? What the hell do I do now?

Through the tears I reach for the spare razor I keep in my glove compartment for emergencies and pull up my sleeve. I need something to clear my mind, and I really tried hard to not let it be this, but right now, I need something.

One, two, three cuts later. Nothing. One, two, three more. Still nothing.

I watch the blood drip down my wrist as my eyes start to well up again.

Focused on the red lines I just drew on my body, trying to keep myself calm. Why was nothing working? Suddenly, almost out of nowhere, it hits me. It's time.

My heart started racing and the tears instantly stopped falling. Of course, nothing was working. This was my opportunity. That last strand of hope I was holding onto has suddenly snapped, and I'm ready.

I roll my sleeve back down and grab onto the steering wheel with the tightest grip I had. Ten and two with shaky hands. I never drive ten and two, but this had to be perfect. Ironically enough, this is probably going to be the safest and most cautious I've ever driven in my entire life.

Slowly, but still shaking, I take my right hand off of the steering wheel and put the car into drive. Just as slowly, I pull back out onto the main road. No music this time. I couldn't have any noise distracting me; I needed to take advantage of the opportunity I've waited so long for. I start to pick up speed as I make sharp turns and drive over potholes, building myself up to the moment that would end it all.

The point of no return. The second that would change everything. Around each turn I picked up speed, driving faster and faster like I was playing a video game. Only this wasn't a video game, and I only have one life.

After a few minutes I stop to catch my breath, which I just realised I had been holding this whole time. I close my eyes for a minute to try and collect myself. Tori, you can do this. This is what you've been waiting for. This is what you want. This is what you need. Okay, I'm ready now. I open my eyes and there it was, right in front of me. A bend in the road with a large tree off to the side, staring at me, calling my name. Okay, this is it.

I put my hand to my heart to feel is beat one last time. I unbuckle my seatbelt as one, single tear rolls down my cheek. Was it out of sadness or happiness? I don't know, and honestly, I don't care. I am ready to go regardless. I'm coming, Pop.

Without a second thought, I slam on the gas with all of my might. Flying like the wind and trying to keep control of the steering wheel, I brace myself for what's about to happen. I start to close my eyes but fight as hard as I can to keep them open. Like I said, this has to be a perfect, dead-on hit. I get to the bend, take in one final breath, and jolt the steering wheel all the way to the left. Within a second, the world turned black, and for a millisecond, I felt my spirit lift up out of my body as I crashed into an obscure destination to Heaven.

Chapter Nine
Morning, Sunshine

Everything was still black, but a different kind of black than before. This time it was a deeper black, but I was relieved by the sight of nothing. I did kind of think things were going to be whiter, though. Maybe I'm in Hell? That would suck, I really wanted to see Pop. I'll just wait, maybe it will change. I guess I never really thought about what to expect. I was too focused on actually doing it.

My thoughts were interrupted by some weirdly loud noises. They almost sounded like robots or computers or something. Should I try to move? Should I try to say something? I opened my mouth but I couldn't get anything out. Before I could try to move on my own, something moved me. My body was moving all on its own. Finally, it's happening, and the white light I was hoping for slowly started to creep into my line of vision and take over my pupils. As it turns out, it wasn't the white light I was actually hoping for.

As I'm fully exposed to the light, I start to feel sick. The whiteness fades and suddenly I see where those weird noises were coming from. Surrounding me was machines, people and monitors. Suddenly, it hits me: I'm still alive. I realise that I'm actually in a hospital room and the darkness that I woke up to was from being inside of the cat-scan machine. Was I feeling sick because I was still alive or because now, I have to deal with the aftermath of a failed suicide attempt? I have no idea.

Probably both.

Before I knew it, the double doors in front me slowly started to creep open. I started to try and sit up but a male nurse quickly approached my stretcher and grabbed onto the sides.

"Hold on tight, we're goin' for a little ride."

His southern accent caught me off guard. I could tell he was trying to be funny but I couldn't get myself to fake a laugh or a smile right now. While I'm being wheeled through the hospital hallways, I'm still feeling sick and my mind is racing. I have no idea what's going to happen next. I didn't exactly plan for this. What are my parents going to say? How are people going to look at me? Or even treat me? My frantic thoughts are interrupted by the nurse pushing me.

"Here we are, darlin'."

I look up and see a young man smiling at me. On his scrubs was a nameplate with the word "Kevin" etched into it. Outside of my room was another hospital worker sitting in a chair right by my door. He nodded at me as I was wheeled into my room.

"Who's the man sitting outside?" I asked Kevin, trying to whisper to ensure that the man outside couldn't hear me.

"That's Derek. He is here to keep an eye on you, hun."

"What do you mean?"

Kevin looked at me with a sad look on his face.

"We found the razors in your car. And saw the cuts and scars on your arms and legs. He's here to make sure you're okay. As we all are, little missy. But he is going to be keeping a special eye on you."

His voice started crack when he noticed a tear roll down my cheek and a look of embarrassment come across my face. He started doing something to the gurney, I think locking it in place or something, probably so he wouldn't have to look at my tears and my facial expression anymore. He could have just said suicide watch.

He walked away to go to talk to Derek when I didn't say anything in response. I just wanted to get in bed, fall asleep and hope to wake up and realise this was all a nightmare. I started to get up off the stretcher when Kevin rushed back over to me.

"Don't move, little lady! You can't move on your own yet!"

I froze up instantly and looked under the blanket. My left arm is in a sling and my stomach is all wrapped up.

"You broke your wrist and a couple of ribs, kiddo."

I guess he could tell that I didn't remember. I guess I was in such shock when I woke up that I didn't even feel the pain. I definitely do now though. Ouch.

Kevin started to slowly help me up off the gurney and into the bed and I threw up. Gross. Stupid broken ribs. After he cleaned me up and shattered the last tiny shred of dignity I had, we tried again. This time I got up high enough to make it onto the bed, but not without some serious pain, and not without getting a good look at myself in the mirror first too. My hair was dirty and pushed back, and across my forehead was a long, ugly, and very red scar. Great, something else about myself to hate and feel self-conscious about.

"How bad is my head?" More tears started coming as soon as I began to utter the words out of my mouth.

"Twelve regular stitches, four internal stitches. Luckily for you we have a plastic surgeon here who was able so stitch you up otherwise it would definitely look a lot worse."

Worse? This looks pretty damn bad and ugly to me. I lifted my good arm and ran my index finer across my forehead to feel the stitches. My hand was shaking when Kevin took notice.

"You know, the police officers who found your car said that this accident was fatal. Honestly, they are absolutely stunned that you made it out of that accident alive. They don't know how you survived it."

I couldn't keep it together anymore. I know he was trying to make me feel better, but I just couldn't control the tears and they just kept coming.

"You're really lucky to be alive, darlin'. I know you're probably not happy about it, but it truly is a miracle. You should be very thankful. You've been given a second chance that not too many people get. And now you have the chance to get yourself some help."

I looked at him with no other response than tears. It's hard to be thankful when all I wanted to do is die. It's hard to be thankful when all I can do is be anxious about what's going to happen next. He put his hand on my shoulder to try and comfort me.

"You're going to be okay, hun. We got you. We will be sure of it."

He took a pause as I embraced his comfort, and then went on to say the most anxiety-inducing, scary sentence I was afraid of.

"Your parents will be here soon."

Kevin left the room, and I just kept on crying. Why was I crying? There were plenty of things to be crying about in that moment. Was it because I wasn't successful? Was it because I was afraid to now deal with the aftermath of this failure? I didn't have the energy to contemplate it. I close my eyes, let out some hard, final tears, and fell into a medicated, depressed sleep. The whole time with Derek watching me, of course.

Chapter Ten
Don't Leave Me, Daddy

Almost as soon as I fell asleep, I was woken up by someone who I never thought I'd see again: my mom. She looked down at me and tears fell from her face onto me. I immediately started tearing up myself, and through the painful, broken gasps of air I could manage to get through my busted ribs, I whisper "I'm sorry," She collapses on top of me and puts all her might into a hug. I didn't even care about the pain in my ribs, but as I look over her shoulder, the sight slaps me in the face. There was my dad, standing inside the doorway, right next to Derek. I squint through my tears and see that he too was crying. The only other time I've ever seen my dad cry is when my Pop died.

My mom finally releases her grip on me and motions for my dad to come over. They both sit down in the chairs besides my hospital bed and the anxiety gradually builds up and punches me in the gut. This should be a fun conversation.

"I don't know what to say," Dad said as he threw up his hands and stands up along with them. He paced around the room and could barely even look at me.

Mom reaches over to grab my hand and chimes in next. "Honey, why?"

What a complex question with so many layers of answers. How was I supposed to answer that? My deepest, darkest truth would destroy her. After what I guess what a long pause, she spoke up again.

"I mean, we knew you were struggling, but this? This is a whole new level."

She's right, they did know I was struggling, but I was very selective about what they knew. I tried to find words to say, but when I opened my mouth to speak, nothing came out. This time, she didn't speak up. It was clear that she would have sat there all day and just waited for an answer.

"You wouldn't understand." Wow, just getting out those three words was tough and painful, both physically and emotionally. I really couldn't talk. Literally.

"Well, get us to understand!" Dad shouted back at me.

I jumped a little and was startled, but I couldn't do anything other than just look at them. I would never get them to understand. First of all, it's impossible to understand unless you're living in it. Second of all, I would never do that to him or my mother, or frankly, anyone. I would never wish the pain and the thoughts that go on in my head on my worst enemy, so how could I tell them? I don't know if I could even if I wanted to; how could I put all of it into words? Regardless, I wasn't going to break their hearts even more. I'd rather them be mad at me than mad at themselves for not being able to help their daughter, even though nothing is their fault.

"You realise you are going to have to get help, don't you?" Finally, I can speak a little easier.

"I know. I'll go to the school psychologist whenever I get out of here." Mom and Dad looked at each other in sync, and then slowly back at me.

"It's not that simple, Tori," Mom started. "You are on suicide watch. Once you are physically able to, you have to go to an inpatient program at a mental hospital for a couple of weeks."

Immediately, I burst out into tears. I definitely knew on some level that this was a possibility, but hearing it out loud made it real, and hearing it from her really got to me.

"Don't let them take me," I begged through tears and fear.

"We don't have a say in this, honey. It's mandated by the hospital," Mom says quietly with a haunting look of desperation on her face.

I look over at Dad and he's still pacing as the doctor walks in. I couldn't read his name-tag through my tears, but honestly, I really didn't care what the hell his name was. I hated him. I hated this hospital. If they think they are helping me by locking me up against my will, they're wrong. If anything, this will make me want to try killing myself all over again, and that will be on them.

Mom walked over to talk to the doctor when I noticed another tear roll down Dad's cheek. Just seeing him cry was enough to bring me to tears.

"Don't leave me, Daddy," I begged softly through the tears and gasps for air.

"Tori, what do you think you did? You tried to leave me, and now you're asking for me not to leave you?"

I was completely dumbfounded. I was not expecting that reaction. I could sense the sadness in his voice but I could also sense the hint of anger he was trying to hide. He walked away towards Mom and the doctor and I just lay there, staring at the ceiling, not sure what to think. I cried myself back to sleep while listening to the voices of my parents and the doctor talking about what they were going to do with me, like I was some plague they couldn't handle. Please God: don't let me wake up.

Part Two
Present

Chapter One
Day Four – C Stands for Crazy

St Vincent's Mental Hospital: Yikes.

I woke up really early this morning. Like before the sun early. I'm not sure why, but sleep just continued to allude me all night. Counting the bumps on the ceiling helps put me to sleep but staying asleep is another challenge all on its own.

After about two weeks of being in the regular hospital, I was transferred here.

This mental hospital was the only place that had an open bed for me, but they couldn't commit me until my ribs were healed up enough for me to walk and do things on my own. Honestly, I was hoping they'd never heal.

The building is pretty boring looking. Nobody wants to be at a mental hospital, the least they could do is try to make it look welcoming and not so hospital-like. Grey walls, white ceiling; real original there, St Vincent's. Since I was being transferred from a medical hospital, I had to be brought in here by an ambulance, so I didn't even really see the front of the building. I'd bet you twenty bucks though that it's got grey walls and white ceilings.

The hospital has a bunch of units that vary depending on diagnosis and age. I remember passing by a lot of them when I was being wheeled through the halls. The same grey wall, white ceiling theme continued into my unit. The only difference was that as soon as you are allowed into the unit through the second set of double doors, there's a big, colourful banner that reads: "Welcome to Ward C" and all of the people who work in the unit signed their name on it. Yeah, that makes me feel more comfortable and happier to be here. NOT. At least they tried harder than the entrance of the building I came through a few days ago, though.

The first few days that I've been here, I had to be on a constant suicide watch. For 48 hours, I had someone with me at all times, just like I did at the regular hospital right after the accident. In this hospital, though, they really watch you. I'm talking, like a hawk. And there were so many different people with me that I don't remember all of their names. Some of them tried to talk to me and keep things somewhat normal, and others just sat there and stared like creeps. Some of them seemed nice and a little more relaxed, and others seemed like they were just waiting for me to try and escape or attempt suicide. The only time there weren't eyes directly on me was when I was in the bathroom. Even then, there was a woman with me facing the corner. You ever try to pee in front of someone in your late teens? It's awkward as hell.

I am off of suicide watch now, but that's only because the hospital is short staffed. I can understand that, though. Not many people can handle this type of job, and not many people even want this kind of job. I can't blame those people, really.

I haven't really spoken much of a word to anyone. I mean, I say hello and goodbye and stuff but nothing of substance or importance. The nurses bring me breakfast, lunch and dinner. They tell me when it's my turn to shower. They tell me every single time there's group therapy or some kind of bonding activity. I've politely declined each and every invitation to those. I'm just not there yet.

They also tell me when it's time to take my medication. I met with a psychiatrist the first day I got here. Again, I didn't really say much, but I guess whatever I did was enough to give me a drugged-up cocktail of different medications. Something for the depression, something for the anxiety, something to curb the self-harm addiction and something to help decrease the suicidal thoughts. They watch me take medications and make me open my mouth and show them that the pills aren't hidden under my tongue. I'm not sure why I would do that, though. Do they think that I don't want to get better? Do they think I like being this way and not having a purpose to live? They clearly don't know what it's like inside my head, obviously. No one does.

Ward C is really small; I'm thinking the smallest unit in the building. I don't know anyone here yet, but besides me, there are only four other kids. I asked one of my "babysitters" why the unit is so small. Don't get me wrong, the less people the better for me, but I was just curious. He told me that Ward C was for "very special cases". Really dude? You could have just told me the most severe, suicidal cases. I wouldn't have been offended. I guess the "C" in the Ward C stands for crazy.

I haven't been able to write in so long. I was on so many pain meds in the other hospital that most of the time I could barely form a coherent sentence, never mind write. Thank God I didn't break my right wrist.

It's been a few days since I've even had a pen and paper in here. Getting things through this door is one of the hardest things, you'd think the President is in here or something. Seriously though, I just wanted to write, but in here, they won't give me anything because everything is "a danger". They're afraid that we'll stab ourselves with the pencils. They're afraid we'll eat the ink out of the pen. I'm not really sure what the big, dramatic fear of paper is? Intentional paper cuts, maybe? Whatever. Screw them, I got it anyway. Luckily, I was able to swipe some from the evaluation desk in the intake room with no one noticing.

These first few nights I've had a room all to myself, which has been nice. No one to have to share space with or make meaningless, uncomfortable small talk with. I just got word from the nurse who brought me breakfast this morning though that I am going to get a roommate any day now. Apparently, her name is Mikayla and she's being transferred here from another mental hospital. I wonder why.

Maybe they didn't know how to help her? Maybe she was fighting with the other patients and causing problems? Or maybe they just didn't want her there because they couldn't handle her? I don't know. Not sure what to expect with that, but hopefully it's not too bad. She better not be a tattletale who's going to rat me out about having a pen and paper in here. All I've been doing is writing since I was able to get my hands on them. If they get taken away because of her, there is going to be a huge problem.

A few minutes later I heard one of the nurses coming down the hallway and I stashed my pen and paper under my pillow so fast. Thank goodness, because he was coming in my room.

"Curfew Tori. Lights off. Oh, and by the way, Mikayla is coming tomorrow. She should be here by lunchtime."

I said nothing, as usual, and he shut the lights. Great, this should be fun. Welcome to Ward C, Mikayla.

Chapter Two
Day Five - It's All
About Mikayla

"Among the crowd, I hustle and bustle through thousands of people. I'm afraid to look back, but I know if I don't, I'll always wonder what I would have seen. Quickly, I jolt my head back, and there he is, chasing me through Grand Central station like a moth being drawn to a light. My legs feel weak, and my feet are tired, but I know that I can't stop. Breathing heavily, I duck into a corner, hoping to become invisible from his vision. Standing as still as a statue, I feel him cross my presence. I see him stop, look around, and then take off again in a hurry. I let out a sigh of relief, not knowing what was to happen next. He turns back, and I feel his gaze staring hard at me. I knew that I was cornered, that I was found, and for that split second I felt my heart stop."

I felt myself jolt up out of my bed, and almost out of my body. It felt like an out of body experience. I sprang up from my bed, realising that I had fallen asleep. Damn, what kind of a crazy nightmare was that? Who is he? My ex? Or was it Kevin or Derek, from the other hospital? Or maybe one of the male "babysitters" I had here? The man didn't really have a face; it was more of a dark, shadowy figure. Could it have been my mental illness chasing me? I felt panic throughout my body through shakes and hyperventilation. I was trying to calm down and recover when I see something out of the corner of my eye. A short girl with longish black, curly hair and dark brown eyes, wearing a hospital outfit and twirling her thumbs sat on the bed next to me. She didn't even seem to notice that I was having a mini panic attack and woke up in a crazy, screaming fit. Either that, or she didn't care.

I'm so not good at picking up social cues, especially awkward ones. Do I say something? Do I leave it alone? Do I act like she's invisible like she's acting towards me? In this social situation, I think it would be more uncomfortable if I said nothing.

"Sorry. Bad dream."

She looked up at me with a blank stare. Nothing but silence.

"What time is it?" What a stupid, random question, but I couldn't think of anything else to say.

Again, nothing but silence. This is so weird. I looked up at the clock that read 2:16 pm. Damn, I slept all morning? I guess it needed it. I haven't slept well since I've been here. During this little conversation I'm having with myself in my head, this girl is still just staring at me, so what am I supposed to do? I just stared back at her, and then eventually down to her feet when the eye contact became too uncomfortable. Well, this is officially awkward. I don't know what exactly happened, but after about thirty seconds or so, her face seemed to light up and she spoke with a gentle a smile across her face.

"I'm Mikayla," she exclaimed, out of nowhere. That was weird.

"Tori," I said with a soft smile, still confused as to what just happened that changed her mind and got her to start talking to me.

"Why not Victoria?"

Huh, was not expecting that.

"I don't know. My sister called my Tori when I was baby, and I guess it just stuck." She said nothing. Again. What is with this girl?

"Or maybe I'm not 'Queen-like' enough to be a Victoria," I quickly added, and immediately, she spoke up. Again.

"No, that can't be right. Queen Victoria's first name was actually Alexandrina. Victoria was actually her second name, now more commonly known as her middle name."

Well, that kept with the theme of this conversation. Again. Unexpected. "I didn't know that. You're pretty smart."

"I was in school studying history before I came here. Secondary education history. I wanted to teach adults in a prison. You know, prisoners who are trying to get their GED's. I wanted to help people better themselves." It was weird; she was talking about this so passionately, yet the tone of her voice made it sound like she had given up.

"That's pretty cool. You can still do that when you get out of here, you know." I know it's kind of hypocritical, but as someone who's not so hopeful, I was trying to give her hope.

"Nah. It's all just a pipe dream now. It wasn't a total loss though. Like, I learned a lot of history buff jokes. Check this one out. 'Civil War jokes? I'm not General-Lee a fan of them.'"

She chuckled to herself, but I just sat there for a second trying to figure out how to react. The polite thing to do is of course laugh, but it's been such a big gap of time now that I think I missed my window. Thanks, social anxiety. I guess she could tell I didn't really understand the joke or know what to say because she cut off my train of thought.

"Okay, well, you'd be laughing if you were a history nerd like my classmates. So, what are you into?"

Huh, what am I into? Depression and mental illness have consumed so much of my life and took the joy out of everything, I don't really know. Luckily, I still have the passion for language and the written word.

"Writing."

"That's cool. What do you write about?" The tone in her voice picked up again and she seemed really interested.

"Well, it depends. Sometimes I like to make up stories. Usually about beautiful things happening to good people."

What I didn't say was that I'll never be one of those good people with beautiful things happening to them. I figure that might be too intense for a first meeting. My mind started to wander again but her gaze of interest snapped me back into the conversation.

I continued on.

"Lately though, I've been writing a lot about me. What I'm feeling, what I'm thinking. Writing has always been my go-to outlet when I'm sad or stressed. Which lately is all the time." I'm not sure why, but I felt comfortable talking to her.

"Does it work?"

"Sometimes."

"So, what happens if it doesn't work?"

I felt her eyes travel and begin to fixate on my arm. I did not need to answer that question. She already knew the answer. The hospital shirt I was wearing wasn't long sleeved. My cuts and scars began to burn and tingle and my hand started to gravitate towards my arm, but was cut off by my low mobility. Stupid, broken arm. I hate this dumb cast. I'm sure she could tell what was going on, but she kept going.

"That's why you're here, right?" she asked, still focusing on my arm. "Amongst other things."

"Like what?"

I don't know why I was so comfortable talking to this girl, but I didn't feel like I had to hide anything or pretend to be something I'm not. I spend every day of my life faking a smile and saying all the right things, it was nice to just be myself and not feel judged about who I am.

"I tried to kill myself."

Wow, I haven't actually said it out loud yet. It feels weird, like it just made the whole thing real.

"Is that where you got that gnarly scar from?" Gnarly. There's a word I haven't heard in a while. Not sure I would describe it as gnarly. Maybe 'ugly' or 'pathetic', but not 'gnarly'. I just nodded at her.

"And that's why your arm is in a cast too, right? What happened?"

"Car accident."

"Wow, that's wild. You've got some balls, girl." I never thought I'd be getting props for attempting to take my own life, but I guess I'll take it.

"Yeah. So why are you here?" Time to change the conversation and take the focus off of me.

"Mood swings."

"That's it?"

"Everyone else calls them 'schizophrenic episodes'. You know, tomatoes, to-mat-toes, that kind of thing. I just refer to them as extreme mood swings."

Schizophrenia. I guess I could see that.

"What happens?" I asked nervously. Maybe she doesn't want to talk about it, especially with a stranger. Stupid question, Tori.

"I don't know how they start; I never quite remember. One minute I'm okay, reading a biography about Amelia Earhart, and the next minute those damn voices start screaming in my ear and I just go crazy. Telling me to do this bad thing and hurt that person. Then eventually they shut up and I go back to my book. See, mood swings."

Wow, I did not know how to respond to that. I just kind of nodded at her again and sat there taking in all of that information when she started again.

"Yeah, people think I'm crazy, but I'm really not." Boy, do I know that feeling all too well.

"You're not crazy. Just different. Like me."

"Thanks. You're pretty cool. I'm glad we're roommates." Cool? Me? I've never been called "cool" before in my life.

"Yeah, me too," I said back with a little half-smile. She smiled back at me as one of the hospital workers showed up in our doorway.

"Mikayla, it's time for one-on-one." Mikayla stood up from her bed and looked right at me.

"I'll see you later, Tori."

"See ya." I replied back. She and the nurse both walked out, and I'm left there alone in my own thoughts. I haven't had a friend in such a long time, I almost forgot what it felt like. To have someone who is going through this hospital stuff too. It's comforting. I reach for my pen and paper under my pillow and start to write. My creative juices are flowing and the words just come naturally. Finally, some good inspiration in a really long time.

"She's carries herself with poise, floating as graciously as an angel among Heaven's clouds. Her presence absorbs all positive energy around her and her aura projects it into society, making the world a better place without even lifting a finger. Walking hand in hand with the spirit of God, she comes over to me, introducing herself as I stand there, frail and timid. Intimidation strikes me as she questions every aspect of my life. I quiver, afraid to say the wrong thing. She turns, and I hide myself away in shame, praying she doesn't choose to come back. Why would she? I am nothing. She will learn that soon enough. She comes back, continuing the conversation revolving around me. Fragile, I stand there and shake, hoping she wouldn't notice. Who knew that this conversation that I so much loathed at the time was with someone I could actually call a friend? Who knew that this one awkward interaction could possibly lead to a life-long relationship? Who would have ever guessed that this unlikely encounter could actually be the start of some kind of friendship?"

Chapter Three
Night Five - Code Orange

"Her presence was one that's hard to describe. Her body said 'bad-ass mother fucker' while her eyes said 'melancholy, frail outsider'. Her black hair was pin straight, and her red bangs hid her right eyebrow and the top of her eyelid. I counted thirteen tattoos and twelve piercings, and that only includes whatever was visible to the naked eye. Who knew what was hidden under her leather jacket, ripped jeans and spiked, motorcycle boots? While absorbing her presence, the tattoo on her forearm struck me. It was an unfinished Japanese sleeve, but it looked like it hadn't been touched in ages. The lotus flowers were blue and purple, slightly hidden behind a Koi fish, consisting of different shades of orange. It was surrounded by turquoise waves, splashing up onto his tail. Within the water was a Daruma doll, drowning under both the crashing ocean and the rest of the image. A disturbing image, watching the good luck of the doll drown under one of life's natural resources. It stared back at me like I had done something wrong. Suddenly, she vanished, and our gaze was broken."

My eyes open quickly and I'm staring at the ceiling. I'm left lying in bed, analysing the dream I just had like it's a school paper. Who was that woman? I swiftly jump out of bed, strip myself of my hospital gown and pyjamas, and recount my tattoos.

The word Strength — One.

Angel Wings — Two.

Italian Infinity Symbol — Three.

Butterfly — Four.

Breast Cancer Ribbon — Five.

Song Quote — Six.

Sun — Seven.

Semi-Colon — Eight.

Anchor and Ribbon — Nine.

Heart Monitor — Ten.

Molecules — Eleven.

Paw Print — Twelve.

Cross — Thirteen.

Writing — Fourteen.

Sugar Skull — Fifteen.

Ladybug — Sixteen.

Mermaid — Seventeen.

Wave — Eighteen.

Who was she? Was she me? Could she be me from the future? I've been having the weirdest dreams since I got here.

Some dreams, some nightmares, but none of them seem to make much sense. I wonder if it could be the medication. Or just my mind going completely insane. That makes sense. A lot of kids may come to this place because they are "insane", but I'm sure a lot of kids come here and this place makes them insane, so that wouldn't surprise me.

I look up at the clock and it reads 12:12 am. Still slightly confused but too tired to give it much more thought at the moment, I get redressed and sluggishly get on the uncomfortable mattress and under the boring, grey comforter. Back in bed, I close my eyes, but they don't seem to want to stay shut. Physically and emotionally, I am so exhausted, but mentally, my mind is racing. Frustrated with my own brain (as usual), I start counting the bumps on the ceiling.

One. Two. Three. Four.

I look over to my right, staring at the vacant bed next to me. The black sheets were all wrinkled and bunched up while the pillows were on the floor accompanied by a plain grey comforter. Her side of the room was exactly the way it was earlier when she went to meet with the therapist. Come to think of it, she hasn't come back in the room since then, and that was a while ago. I don't know where they took her, or what they did to her, and while I of course felt for the girl, it was kind of nice to have a room to myself. After having my own room at home, it was weird to have to share my space, especially with a stranger. Don't get me wrong, I like Mikayla, and I am in no way judging her for her mental health issues. I've only had one conversation with the girl but I feel very comfortable talking to her. Like she can understand me, or at least relate to me, more than anyone I have ever met before.

I go back to counting the bumps on the ceiling. Five. Six. Seven. Eight.

My counting is interrupted by the screams piercing through the walls. That was nothing new here, really. With the walls being so padded, you'd think they'd be soundproof. But then again, how could they be soundproof? The nurses needed to know what was going on in each room 24/7. "Unstable" they called us; apparently, we needed babysitters. There's no privacy here.

I try to distract myself by beginning to count again. Nine. Ten. Eleven. Twelve… Or was that Eleven? Dammit, I have to start again.

One. Two. Three. Four. "Code orange!"

Holy crap, that damn loudspeaker scared the shit out of me. "I repeat, code orange!"

Well, that's definitely new. What the hell does that mean? I spring out of bed and slip my boring grey robe on. I wasn't going in the hallway in just my T-shirt and shorts; I didn't plan on really going outside my room, but just in case, I couldn't risk letting the other kids see me. I slide my feet in my even more boring grey slippers, slightly open the door and take a peek into the hall.

Oh, so there was my roommate. I still don't know her all too well, but I do know what schizophrenia is, and the way she is acting right now is nothing like she was acting this morning. Maybe she's bipolar too? Honestly, the way she's freaking out on the outside right now is what I feel happening to me on the inside. The difference is she just can't control it and keep it on the inside, she has to express it outwardly. I'm sure medication can help control that, and I'm sure she's on some kind of medication cocktail, just like me and every other patient in here.

Her scream sent a chill down my spine as she caught my eyes. Honestly, her stare was terrifying. Like she was looking through me, expecting me to help and make everything better. Honestly, like if I couldn't do those things, that she was going to kill me.

It took thirty minutes, but she finally stopped screaming and calmed down, thanks to three huge men and a long medical needle. The way she was fighting off these three men, she was a tough girl. She doesn't look like she can be that strong, but I guess when you're being screamed at by voices in your head, you're determined to do whatever it is they tell you. Poor Mikayla. She can't help it. I'm sure she feels trapped and dictated by the voices. Like she can't escape the hell, trauma and fear within herself. I don't have schizophrenia, but I do know what it feels like to just want to break out of yourself like that.

I close the door, knowing that Mikayla would not be coming back tonight. I remove my boring grey robe and slip out of my even more boring grey slippers, and climb back into bed. I wrap myself in my comforter, hoping it would protect me from the hell outside my room that I couldn't seem to escape from. It can't protect me from myself, but then again, nothing can, not even this place.

I go back to counting. One. Two. Three. Four. Nine more days.

Five. Six. Seven. Eight. Just nine more days.

Chapter Four
Day Six – Hello, Sweetheart

I've never been much of a talker. I prefer to think. To write. To dream. It's always better suited me to let my thoughts and emotions out in more of a silent way. A way in which I had an outlet for my feelings but did not have to risk the judgement or vulnerability that comes with other people knowing. They are still being psycho jerks about giving me a way to write though. Writing is a healthy outlet, it's unfortunate that they can't give us that opportunity. I guess those ways to hurt yourself with a pen, a pencil and paper could be plausible, if you're really that determined and unhappy, either here or in regular day life, but I think the real reason that they won't give us those things is because they think if I can't write what I am thinking and feeling that I will be more inclined to talk to someone. Well guess again, Ward C. People sneak things in here all the time, I've proven that myself.

Whether I felt comfortable with it or not, I knew it was just a matter of time before I was forced to see the one-on-one therapist here. The office was exactly as you'd expect it to be. The walls were egg-shell white and the floor was covered in a stained beige carpet. I guess they wanted to deviate from the "black and grey" theme of the rest of the hospital. I guess that they wanted the room to be a bit brighter than the rest of the place. Maybe give off some kind of positive aura? I don't know. It kind of made me anxious though. Welcome back, my old friend. Honestly though, "white and beige" are just a different kind of a boring than "black and grey" in my opinion. There were a few signs on the wall, like inspirational or motivational type phrases, like the kind you see in elementary school classrooms. "If you dream it, you can do it" and "you can have excuses or results, but not both". That was enough for me; moving on.

The furniture was mostly dark. The desk and chairs were brown, but so brown that they were pretty much almost black. There was even one of those chaise lounge things that you see in the movies. You know what I mean, where the patient is supposed to lay down and spill everything dark and depressing that's ever happened in their entire life. And then when the patient was done rambling, the therapist would say "So how do you feel about that?" Yeah, no thanks. I'll take a brown-black chair. Like I said, it was exactly as you'd expect.

As I waited for the doctor, I took notice of the sticker, prominently stuck on the inside of the also egg-shell white door. In bold, black letters, it read the word "Safe zone" with a red checkmark next to it. First of all, if this was a "safe zone", it wouldn't be in a mental hospital. The doctor literally has to tell everyone in the building who "resides over your case" what you said. Second of all, how do you expect me to feel safe when I'm being forced to talk to this person, by myself, against my will? Yeah, that really makes me feel safe. The whole sticker is just an elaborate oxymoron, really.

Honestly, I don't know how or why people expect me to be into this whole therapy thing. If I won't talk to people I know about my problems and feelings and whatever, what makes anyone think that I will be open to talking to a complete stranger?

My thinking is interrupted when I hear the door start to creak open. Here comes the anxiety again. Good to see you again, buddy.

"Tori? Hi. I'm Dr S. It's very nice to finally meet you. I've heard so much about you."

Great, what kind of things did she hear? That I attempted suicide and I don't want to be in this hospital or talking to you? Wonderful start. I just looked at her, not really knowing how to respond or react. Her voice was gentle, yet strong. Just like the room. Exactly as you'd expect it.

Dr S was tall. Like damn, she definitely did not need to be wearing those heels. They were black, spiked heels, at least six inches high. They also looked like Jimmy Choo shoes, at least a few hundred bucks. And that didn't even look like the most expensive thing on her body. Between those shoes, the Gucci coat and the Prada handbag, I don't know what was most expensive. I doubt she could be making that much money working here. I wonder why she took this job.

"So, what's going on, sweetheart?" Her term of endearment did not lighten the mood. Also, I'm no professional, but that doesn't sound like the best way to kick off a therapy session. Just saying.

"I'm fine." I looked off into the distance, trying to get back to where my thoughts were taking me before they were so rudely interrupted by Dr S. I wonder what the "S" stood for anyway. Silverman? Could it be her first name? Maybe Sharon? Again, my thoughts were interrupted.

"There is no need to be embarrassed. Tell me what happened, sweetheart."

Sweetheart #2. I know she knew what happened, she read my file. My head dropped a bit as I let out a sigh. We sat in silence for a few minutes, making awkward eye contact every thirty seconds or so. I learned this thing that if you look in the middle of someone's forehead that to the other person, it actually looks like you are looking in their eyes, making eye contact. That usually helps when my good friend anxiety shows up, but not so much this time. I don't know how much time went by, but it felt like quite a bit. I know that if I don't say something soon, she would ramble on about how I can trust her and something like "hey, look at the sticker, this is a safe zone!" And I just don't feel like hearing all that again.

"You know what happened," I mutter, still looking down.

"Yes, but I do not know why. So why don't you tell me?" she spoke soft and gentle, but at the same time, it sounded like she was almost pleading to me, begging me to open up.

"I don't want to do this. I am fine now, really," I had lied again, and I knew she knew that. She wouldn't understand though, not really. Just because she studied mental illness does not mean she gets what's going on inside of my head and heart. If you haven't lived it, don't say you get it because most people are just curiously ignorant. My thoughts were interrupted, yet again.

"Clearly you're not though, sweetheart, otherwise you wouldn't be here." Sweetheart #3. She was right, obviously, but I could not admit that to her.

"It's not easy living like this, and I'm sick of it. People need to respect that I am a grown woman who can make her own decisions and if I don't want to be here, I shouldn't have to feel guilty about it." Each word was complemented with a weak, melancholy tone of voice, and I felt myself trembling. With all of my might I tried to fight off the tears, but I slowly lost that battle when I saw how she looked at me. She gave that classic look. A look that said "Oh you poor thing, but I am going to continue to torture you for the next 53 minutes." Luckily, I was wrong.

"Let's pick this up next time, okay? Why don't you go get some rest, sweetheart?"

Sweetheart #4. Really, all that for nothing? She just pried me open a tiny bit and she's just going to let me go? Fine by me. If I knew that's what it took to get this to end, I would have started off with that. I stood up, not saying another word, but nodding in agreement even though I don't have any intention of picking this up next time. I want to get better, I swear I do, but I don't think this is the way to help me. I headed for the door when I heard her sweet, soft voice chime in again.

"Oh, Tori, before you go…"

I should have known it wouldn't have been that easy.

"I have a little assignment for you. I heard you're a good writer and I can see that you're not big into the whole talking thing. We meet again in four days. Before then, I want you to write three suicide notes. One to your parents and one to someone of your choosing. Maybe someone that you really care about. Or maybe even someone who you feel contributed to your feelings of wanting to not be here anymore." Huh, what an interesting concept. Maybe Dr S isn't all expensive handbags and height.

"And the third?" I asked.

"And for the third, I want you to write one to yourself. I want you to be totally open and raw and honest in every single one of these letters. I promise, nobody will see these letters but you. I don't even have to read them if you don't want me to, but if you want, I will and then we can discuss what you wrote. If not, we'll discuss how writing them made you feel. Whatever you are comfortable with is what we'll do. I'll arrange for you to get a pen, paper and someone to supervise that you're okay. Sound good?"

I mean it didn't sound amazing, but it definitely sounded better than some other assignments or scenarios. I'm glad and honestly surprised that she's willing to work with me. I nodded back at her and she let out a smile. All of the sudden, I felt the verge of tears. My eyes started to water and I turned around instantly and headed for the door. I did not want her to see me crying. I exit the office and walk through the halls toward my room. As I walk in, the sight of my bed makes me feel somewhat at ease. I lay on my mattress and instantly my eyes start to feel heavy. She was right, I definitely could use some rest after that.

Why was I crying, though? Her smile read to me that she was so happy that she got through to me. Like she was proud of me or something for giving it a shot and being willing to try to get better. Like I said, I do want to get better, and if she lets me write out everything, I feel I can be more honest that way, and maybe actually get some help. Wouldn't that be something.

Chapter Five
Night Six – The Self-Help Book
I'll Never Write

"They say the people who look the happiest are really the people who are the saddest on the inside. Even with that statement being one of the most common unwritten laws of the population, that doesn't make much of a difference within today's society. The cruel and unjust judgement and assumptions made by other people do nothing but cause pain, sometimes so unbearable that the victim feels that they cannot go on any longer. They also say the people who are the saddest on the inside are most likely than not the strongest. The problem with being so strong is that nobody ever asks you if you are okay. But life cannot be handled alone. Whether you're happy or sad, lively or depressed, human interaction and connection is essential to make it through something as complicated as life. Like I said, I'm not really religious anymore, but I did go to Catholic school, and I do know that even Jesus Christ had His 12 disciples. God the Father was cared for and kept by his followers. But who prays for Satan? Who, in so many centuries, has had the humanity to pray for the one sinner who needed it most?

He who asks for help shall receive it. He who asks for love will find it. He who asks for greatness will achieve it. But what about he who is too scared to ask? Does he not deserve to be granted these things just because he's a bit more shy? The fear of rejection overcomes the desire of fulfilment. For those like him who do not know how to ask, should they be left to fend for themselves in this wide world? If they do speak up, even with a shaky voice, what happens if their terror of rejection becomes reality? They tried so hard to trust again, and if you prove their fears right, they will never be able to. He who makes himself vulnerable to rejection still fears it. Don't let those people down. Those who are afraid to ask for help, love and greatness, most likely could use it the most.

Kurt Cobain. Alexander McQueen. Chris Cornell. Chester Bennington. Robin Williams. Avicii. Kate Spade. These are only a few of the many celebrities who have taken their own life. Everyone thought they were famous, rich and happy, but being a celebrity doesn't mean that your life is perfect. There is depression. There is heartache. There is loneliness. No matter who you are.

Most people would say "I can't process this yet" or "I'm still in shock" however sadly for me, the shock factor to suicide and mental health issues no longer greatly affects me anymore.

On the Hollywood scene, the horrific event of suicide happens, the world mourns, and people move on. But what about the families? What about the people who just saw that celebrity as their mother? Their father? Their brother or sister? Their cousin? They live a life wondering why, whether a suicide note is left or not.

Celebrity or not, the families of these people who felt so helpless that they thought the only way out was to take their own life are eternally affected.

Enough is enough. It is time to recognise, for those who haven't already, that mental illness is a real disease, and just because it is an invisible illness doesn't make it any less harmful or potentially fatal. It is time to show the world that we are ready to make a difference and be there for each other.

So, what can the world do? We can band together. We can unite. We can be kind to one another and not enforce the darkness that the world itself thrusts upon society already. We can follow the paths that these celebrities left for us before they reached their lowest point. These people have impacted the world through not only their industry, but through the way they made people feel, and we can do that too. We can change the world; we just need to realise that before this tragedy strikes again."

Why will I never write it? Because I sound like a hypocrite. I mean, who am I for people to believe? I'm basically just one suicidal kid telling other suicidal kids that suicide isn't the answer. I'm living a hypocritical lie of a life. I mean, who would want to read about that? I don't even want to live it.

I hear footsteps from the hall and a feint voice that I couldn't make out.

Quickly, I hid my pen and paper under my pillow and laid down acting as if I was just counting the bumps on the ceiling like I always do.

One. Two. Three. Four.

My counting is majorly interrupted when the voice gets closer and the person responsible appears in the doorway.

"Hey girl, what's up?" Mikayla is back. Not only is she back in the room, but she is back to the Mikayla she was the first time I met her. Not last night's Mikayla. I have no idea who that girl is.

"Hey, how are you?" I replied back. What I really wanted to ask was what the hell happened last night, but I didn't know if that would be too invasive for her, and the last thing I wanted to do was cause another episode.

"I'm better now. Last night was crazy, wasn't it?"

Okay Tori, think about this. If I say yes, it may look like I'm calling her crazy. If I say no, it may look like I'm crazy. Oh geez, welcome back, anxiety.

"Yeah, it was definitely interesting. Are you feeling better now?" I hope that didn't come out wrong.

"Oh, much better." I'm glad she didn't take offense to that. "Well, that's good. What happened?"

"I already told you! I don't really know how they start. They just happen," she snarked back at me. It sounded like I upset her. Oh God, fix this.

"You're right, I'm sorry. I guess I was just wondering if there was a trigger. You know, so you can almost know it's going to happen before it happens and then maybe there are ways to control it. I try to do that sometimes myself."

"To control your urge to cut yourself, you mean?" she questioned. I just realised that I never actually came out and said that to her. But we both knew that she knew, clearly.

"Yes," I looked down at her feet, afraid to meet her eyes after admitting to that out loud. Almost as soon as I do, she walks over to my bed and sits herself down right next to me.

"Hey, it's okay. We all have issues. You should really get to know some of the other people here. Then maybe you wouldn't feel so alone. We all may be alone in our own, sad lives, but here, we are all alone together," she said in the sweetest, most genuine voice.

Wow, that was actually really insightful. I like Mikayla, I trust her. I feel like I can help her, and I even feel like she can possibly even help me too. Today has been a wild ride. I have never felt any type of hope for help before, and today, for some reason, it's happened twice. Maybe this place isn't as horrible as movies and books and society make it out to be. Right as I was about to respond, I was cut off.

"Curfew, girls. Lights off and get in bed," one of the caretakers said from the doorway. Mikayla turned the light off and went back to her side of the room. I got under the covers and turned to face the wall while she changed into her pyjamas. A few tears rolled down my cheek, too. I hear Mikayla get into bed and let out a sigh.

"Hey, Mikayla?"

"Yeah?"

"I'd like to go to group with you tomorrow," I whisper, hopefully loud enough for her to hear me, because I did not know if I could get myself to say it again.

"Good. I'm glad. Goodnight, Tori."

"Goodnight," I whisper back to her. I am proud of myself, for once in my life. I am trying. I am trying to get help. I am trying to be better. It may have taken Dr S and Mikayla to push me there, but I am still doing it. Maybe this will work.

Chapter Six
Day Seven – What Kind of
Healing Circle Is This?

I opened my mouth to speak, but nothing came out. I tried with every fibre of my being to get the words out, but I just couldn't; they were all mixed-up in the mess of my anxious mind. The words are in my head, but not willing to come out, fearful of the consequences. I knew I had to tell someone; he needed to be chastised for his heinous actions. There needed to be consequences for what he did to me. For what he did to the many innocent girls before and after in that classroom. I opened my mouth to speak, but nothing came out. I can't keep this secret any longer. The memories of that day weighed down on my shoulders the way heavy dew rests on morning grass. I can still feel his shadow and the gloom of his presence linger over me. Someone had to know the truth.

"Tori, do you recall the day of March 16th, 2008?"

I opened my mouth to speak, but nothing came out. I tried so incredibly hard not to recall that day.

"Miss?" I opened my mouth to speak, but nothing came out.

In almost the same instant, my nightmare was interrupted and I saw Mikayla standing right over me. Wow, I haven't had a dream about that in a long time.

"Tori, are you okay?"

"Um, yeah, I'm fine. Sorry. Just a bad dream."

"You were shaking and moving around so much, I thought you were going to fall out of bed. What were you dreaming about?" she asked.

"It was nothing."

"Clearly it was something, but we can talk about it later if you want. It's time for group. I'll give you some privacy and wait for you in the hall," she said as she stepped out of the room. Damn, I couldn't believe the morning came as fast as it did. I feel like I didn't sleep at all, but apparently, I slept enough to have that nightmare. I can't think about that right now. I have to focus. Okay Tori. First group. You can do this.

I got dressed quickly and met Mikayla outside of our room in the hallway. "Ready?" she asked me with the biggest smile on her face. She seemed so proud of herself that she was able to convince me to go to group.

"I guess. Here goes nothing," I reply, with a little bit of a half-smile.

Mikayla and I walk down the hall in silence towards the group therapy room.

We walk in and the first thing I notice is more of the inspirational, motivational posters, just like the ones in Dr S' office. More quotes like 'You can overcome anything' and 'Every day is a new day'. Again, that was enough for me; moving on.

In the centre of the room were a bunch of chairs huddled together in a circle. All of the other kids were already sitting around, waiting for the instructor to show up. Mikayla and I went over and sat down in the circle with the group. She began talking to some of the girls, and just as she was about to introduce them to me, a voice came from the doorway.

"Okay gang, quiet down and let's begin," Dr S. I should have known from those damn posters. She walked in and sat in the remaining empty chair, which happened to be directly across from me.

"Tori, welcome to the Ward C Healing Circle. Thank you for joining us. We're all so glad that you finally decided to come listen to and maybe even share with the group."

Silence. I didn't know what to say. Thanks for having me? That's stupid. So, as usual, I went to my signature, awkward 'I don't know what to do right now' gesture, and let out a quick half-smile.

"Tori, would you like to introduce yourself?"

I suddenly snapped out of my thoughts when I heard Dr S's soft, gentle voice. As I snapped back into reality, I realised that everyone's eyes were fixated on me, waiting for me to speak. After what seemed like forever, I mustered up the courage to say something.

"Um, okay… Hi. I'm Tori. I'm from Port Chester, New York, and I am seventeen years old." That was enough for now. Luckily it was, because before I could fit in another word even if I wanted to, one of the girls began shouting.

"Hey, I'm from Rye! We're practically neighbours!" She sounded way too excited, but I gave her a little smile anyway. She seemed happy. I'm not sure if she was happy in general or if that made her so happy, but regardless, good for her. Glad I could make someone happy. There was a small, awkward silence when Dr S chimed in again and broke it.

"Very nice, Tori. Welcome, and thank you. Is there anything else you would like to share with the group?" She sounded like a pre-programmed robot. I looked at her and shook my head no, but that didn't stop the group from asking questions.

"Where did you get that big scar on your forehead?" one of the boys blurted out. I was kind of expecting Dr S to say something like 'Hey, that's rude' or 'Maybe it's personal' but she didn't. Instead, she just let it happen and looked at me for an answer too. Welcome back, anxiety. I missed you… not.

"I tried to kill myself."

Oh my God, why did I say that? Where the hell did that come from? I couldn't have just said it was a car accident? Geez, I'm so stupid. I loathe myself. My anger quickly turned into a loss of emotion or thought. I was numb, empty, and hollow. It was hard enough to admit that to just Mikayla, but to a group of kids I don't even know? Awkward.

"How? By trying to slice your head open?" the same boy asked.

Okay, is this kid serious? The sad part is, he sounded it. But some of the other kids laughed so I'm sure he was just making fun of me.

"Shut up, dipshit, she was in a car accident." Here comes Mikayla to the rescue. She seemed to care more than Dr S. Knowing her, she probably thought it was healthy for me to be honest and have an "open and healthy dialogue" or something. For me, it's just an anxiety attack waiting to happen.

"Hey, language Mikayla!" Oh sure, this she cares about.

"That's stupid. Why not just shoot yourself? Or hang yourself, even? You totally have a much better chance of dying that way." Okay, seriously, what kind of healing circle is this?

"That's enough, Mike." Ah, so the stupid kid has a name. Finally, Dr S decided to step in and say something.

"No, I'm serious. If you really wanted to die, you should have just done something like that. What you did was dumb." He just wouldn't stop.

"That's it, Michael. To the time-out room. Now!" It's about time. You go Dr S.

"Screw you, I'm not going anywhere bitch!" Michael's face turned red instantly like he was going to explode. Something came over him, like the worst thing in the world just happened or his life just ended. He got up fast and picked up the chair he was sitting in like he was going to throw it. Before he could make another move, two male nurses stormed in and dragged him to the time-out room. Whatever that is. I definitely did not want to know. After another awkward silence, Dr S spoke up.

"Tori, are you okay?" she asked, very sincerely, it seemed.

I have no idea. Was I? I honestly have no idea what I was feeling. I should be angry Mike, but I don't get angry at other people often. I'm not really an angry person in general. Usually, my angry has always been turned inwards. Whatever happens, I always blame it on myself. It's always my fault, somehow, some way. All the external anger, I turned inwards and hated myself for. I just looked at her and nodded, but she could tell that I wasn't so sure. Here it comes, the panic attack I was waiting for. And I'm pretty sure Dr S could see it.

"Would you like to be excused from the rest of group today?"

I quickly stood up from my chair and nodded again. Mikayla stood up with me and gave me a hug. I was so numb; I couldn't even hug her back. I went straight to my room and into my bed. I couldn't believe what just happened. Was Mike, right? Did I not try hard enough? In the moment, I just felt it. I just felt it would work. I just felt it was time. I did want to die, more than anyone could ever fathom, so why didn't I do something more fatal? Yeah, screw group. I'll just stick to my writing, thanks.

Chapter Seven
Night Seven - One Small, Mentally Ill Family?

There is a difference between being alone and being lonely. When you're alone, you're in complete solitude. You're physically by yourself. When you're lonely, you're mentally by yourself. Sometimes the two meanings get misconstrued, especially when you're stuck in a mind like mine.

I was surrounded by 3,200 faces in high school every day, and yet I lived my life every day being lonely. It's amazing how easy it is to feel lonely when you're not actually alone. On the rare occasion, someone will ask the standard "Hey, how are you?" question. Now, think about it. I barely know these people. They don't care how I am. But they ask this question because they feel like they have to. They ask it because it's a social construct, so I get it. I go along for the pretend ride and usually respond with the standard "I'm good, thanks, and you?" response. Sometimes they answer with a simple "good", because why would they want to give me details about their life? Again, they don't know me. Other times, they just send a fake smile my way. Regardless of which response they choose, it's chosen to end the conversation quickly and not give a leeway into a new topic.

When someone asks me that question though, it gets me thinking. Huh, how am I? I'm trapped. Lonely. Misunderstood and miserable. Of course, I'd never say that, though. They don't want to give me details of their life because they don't know me, and the feeling is mutual. So again, I go with the typical answer and follow society's social conformities. So yeah, you can say I'm fine. Fine being trapped.

People say that you aren't as lonely when you know someone else who is going through the same things as you. Being locked up in this place, there are lots of people who have been through things like me. Some are of course in a worse situation. Things could always be worse, but generally speaking, I know there are a lot of people who could probably relate to some of my feelings and thoughts. I still can't help but feel lonely, though. I'm scared to open up. My trust issues are so bad, I don't want to give anyone any "ammunition" to use against me. Something that they can someday throw in my face for whatever reason. It's happened too many times before, why risk it? Mikayla and I have begun to grow close, so that's helped somewhat, but still not enough. I'm too afraid to let me guard down this early. I'm sure she's a great person and so far, has shown nothing except for the fact that she is a good friend, but I'm too scared to let my guard down this early. I know better than that by now. Hence the loneliness.

Being lonely can be really scary. This world is huge and daunting and intimidating and you shouldn't have to conquer it and face it alone. Not when there are 7.6 billion people on

Earth. You'd think one would make you feel not so lonely. But I guess not.

My thoughts were interrupted when Mikayla came into the room. She came straight to me and made herself comfortable, getting under the covers and laying in my small, twin-size mattress right next to me.

"You doing, okay?" she asked. Again, just like when it happened this morning, I wasn't really sure.

"I guess so," I answered as I shrugged my shoulders.

"Mike can be a jerk, but it's not totally his fault. He has something called borderline personality disorder. One of the symptoms is a bad temper and mood swings." I knew what borderline personality disorder was. I could see that in him.

"I'm proud of you for coming with me to group today. Thank you." Wow, that was so nice and unexpected. She barely knew me, but was already proud of me? She spoke again too quickly before I could say anything to respond.

"Come on, let's go. Everyone's in the hang out room. I'll introduce you to the rest of the group. It'll be fun," she said as she climbed out of my bed. She just stood there, waiting for me to get up. I gave her a look of uncertainty and she grabbed my arm.

"Come on, Tori, I was just in there with them, it was fine. Come with me." She dragged out her words and pulled my arm loosely like she was joking around with me, but also like she was dead serious and that she would be upset if I didn't go with her. I smirked a little and she could tell that she once again got what she wanted.

"Yay! Let's go," she exclaimed and I started to climb out of bed. She was a good friend; I need to be pushed like that sometimes and get out of my own head. I never really had someone care so much about me to do that and help me like that. Huh, maybe that one who is supposed to make me not feel so lonely is Mikayla.

We got out into the hall and head straight for the hang out room. Mikayla seems so happy and so excited like she did this morning, it's actually very sweet and heart-warming to see. I'm glad I could make her smile. She deserves it, she's been a really good friend to me in here.

We go in the hang out room and everyone is there. As I'm about to walk in with Mikayla, she pauses and grabs my arm to stop me.

"I'm going to give you the low-down first," she said as she nodded over to the left side of the room. On the couch were two girls chatting.

"Over there on the right, that's Jessica. She has bulimia and anorexic tendencies at times. She's a nice girl, but clearly needs a reality check as well as a new mirror and perspective of herself. Next to her is Liv, who struggles a lot like you. Depression and self-harm issues, too, I think. You two would probably get along well together and relate to each other a bit," she took a pause; I think to let me digest all of that information before she continued. Then she nodded towards the TV section, and over there were two boys playing a video game.

"You already know Mike. Borderline Personality Disorder accompanied with severe good looks. Like a deadly, adorable weapon."

Okay, that was odd. But also, not completely untrue. Clearly Mike had some issues and obviously was a jerk to me, but he was cute, I'll give him that.

"Then lastly, we have Andrew. He's usually quiet, but his bipolar disorder can make him into a whole different person sometimes. He seems to follow Mike around. I think he's shy and insecure, but also very sweet. So yeah, that's everyone. We all have issues, and we're all stuck in here together. Let's go."

Here he comes again, my good friend, anxiety. Mikayla and I walk in and head towards the girls.

"Hey guys, what's up?" Mikayla exclaims to them.

"Hi, Mikayla; hi, Tori," Jessica replied in a high, somewhat mouse-like voice. Turns out she's the one who lives in Rye. She seemed like the typical blonde, barbie doll, bimbo kind of girl. Like I always say, though, I don't judge a book by its cover. The only thing I could tell for sure by looking at her is that the girl is skinny. Like very skinny. Like, I'm talking bones sticking out of her body skinny. Poor girl. She's beautiful, and she definitely does not need to be unhealthily skinny like this. I'd like to try and convince her of that.

Next, there's Olivia, but everyone called her Liv for short. She's average height, average body type, with beautiful, pin straight, long brown hair that reached all the way down to nearly her hip bone. She didn't say anything, but I smiled at her and she smiled back. Every time I've seen her, she's been in long sleeves. If Mikayla was right, then I get why. I noticed out of the corner of my eye that one of her sleeves was bunched up a little bit and what peeked out was in fact a self-harm scar. She noticed me noticing quickly and fixed her sleeve. Mikayla and Jessica were already busy talking and in their own conversation, so they didn't notice anything.

Anyway, in my experience, people who don't self-harm don't notice self-harm scars or recognise them as such.

Liv looked so embarrassed, like she was about to go into a full-on panic attack. I felt bad and mouthed 'it's okay'. I pointed at my cast and again mouthed 'me too', just so she knew that she wasn't alone. Her face stayed stoic but I could tell that she knew what I meant. We both had a mutual understanding of what we were going through, and even though we barely knew each other, we were connected and bonded through that simple thirty second moment.

"Hey, do you guys want to turn that stupid video game off and watch a movie or something?" Jessica called out over to the boys. Mike paused the game, turned around to face us and shot a look like Jessica just offended him.

"Hey, video games aren't stupid. It's like living in a different world. I think we all would love to live in a different world other than our own, no?" Mike asked.

"Yeah, they're awesome," added Andrew, following Mike's lead. I don't know what came over me, but I tried to chime in.

"Well then by that logic, movies do the same thing. They take you out of your world for a few hours and transport you into a new one," I added.

"Yeah, but video games are more hands-on. You're actually doing something and making decisions and actions other than just watching, so you're definitely more involved in that world than you are in the world of a movie. Duh," Mike snapped back at me, like I just insulted him and said the dumbest thing ever.

"Let's get back to our video game," Mike barked at Andrew, and the two of them turned around and un-paused the game.

"Okay, did I do something to him? He seems to not like me but I don't know why," I asked the girls. I mean really, what the hell did I do to this guy?

"Actually, Tori, I think it's the opposite," Mikayla said as she looked at the girls and they all shared a smirk.

"What do you mean?"

"You know, it's like in kindergarten. When a boy was mean to you, it meant that they actually liked you," said Liv. That was the first thing I've heard her say since I met her yesterday. To me, that theory never made sense. A boy shouldn't be mean to you if he likes you, that seems counterproductive.

"Yeah, Tori, he likes you!" Jessica chimed in. All of the girls sounded so excited about this and it didn't even make sense to me.

"Yeah, well, we are not in kindergarten. Even if he does like me, I don't think I'm ready yet." I was hoping that would drop the conversation and we could move to something else, but it didn't.

"Not ready because some jerk screwed you over and broke your heart or not ready because you are still planning on killing yourself when you get out of here?" New known fact: Jessica is blunt.

"Jess," Mikayla said as she glanced at her with a look that said "Oh my God why did you just say that?" Liv just sat there, doing what I always do when I am in an awkward or uncomfortable scenario: looking down at her feet.

"Sorry, Tori. I didn't mean for it to come out like that," she said with a sad yet still slightly curious look on her face.

"It's okay." I didn't want to make her feel bad. I know she didn't mean to upset me. I hope Jessica wasn't expecting me to answer that question because honestly, I don't know the answer. Both, maybe? I'm definitely not ready because of that jerk who screwed me over and broke my heart, but I also don't know how I am going to feel when I get out of here. I can only hope that I won't be as on the edge as I clearly was before, but who knows. I'm trying, of course, but I also can't get my hopes up. I've learned that it's better to not have hope because less hope means less disappointment.

"Let's go watch those boys and their dumb video game," Mikayla said, trying to break the awkward moment that was currently occurring. Jessica and Liv got off the couch and followed Mikayla over to the TV section. I followed behind and the four of us sat on the two other couches surrounding the TV. After about five minutes or so of watching them, Jessica spoke.

"Mike, why don't you teach Tori how to play the game?" Okay Jessica, I see what you're doing here. Mike looked at me with a weird look. It wasn't a "I hate you" kind of look, matching the way he's been acting towards me, but instead it was more like a nervous look. I've never seen him like that before. He's always seemed so cool and collected. Before any of us could say anything else, a hospital worker showed up in the doorway.

"Back to your rooms, guys. Time to get ready for bed."

Well, that was close. Saved by the bell. We all got up to head to our rooms and Mike still looked weird.

"Well, maybe next time?" I asked him, trying to cut the tension and help him relax. As soon as I said that, his nervous look faded.

"Sure, no problem. I can teach anyone video games, even you," he responded back. There he was, the normal Mike was back.

"Okay, cool. Goodnight," I said back to him with a little smile.

"Hey, you have dimples! They're cute." Okay, here's weird Mike. I could feel the stares from the all-female peanut gallery behind me as I began to blush.

"Thanks," I replied. I honestly did not know what else to say.

"You're welcome. Goodnight, Tori."

He turned around and walked in the hallway. The second he was gone, the girls all came up to me with looks of "Oh my gosh how cute" and "Oh my gosh he likes you". I was waiting for the bombardment of comments, but they all just stood there with those looks on their faces until Jessica chimed in.

"See?" Jessica asked in a "I told you so" kind of way. I just brushed passed them as I laughed a little.

"Goodnight, guys. See you tomorrow," I said through giggles as I walked back to my room. In my room, I put my pyjamas on and got into bed. Mikayla came in a few minutes after me and did the same.

"So, did you like everyone?" she asked me.

"Yeah, everyone seems nice," I replied.

"Good, I'm glad. We're like one small, mentally ill family."

Huh, I guess we are. Everyone seemed pretty cool, even Mike. We're all going through different problems but we're all going through the same thing here. It's nice to have people who can understand what it's like to be in a place like this. I'm still cautious, though. Like I said, less hope means less disappointment, and I don't know how much more disappointment I can handle in one lifetime.

Chapter Eight
Day Eight – The Breakfast Gang

"She hides in the corner of the room, all alone with nothing but the bottle of vodka lodged tightly in her hand. She's never felt so lonely in her life. Darkness suffocates her presence as she continues to slip farther and farther into the background of her melancholy life. She was waiting to be found, even though she knew nobody would be looking. Or so she thought. Her desire to be noticed does not go unanswered. Drunkenly, she stumbles into the next room, bypasses all of the other partygoers and gives into all social peer pressures. In an altered state of mind, she grabs his hand and leads the way to the bedroom…"

Suddenly I snap out of my nightmare when Mikayla's voice wakes me. "Come on Tori, it's time for breakfast. You're having it with us today!" Breakfast? Normally they just bring me my food here.

That dream, though. It's amazing, how someone so fragile and lonely could be so convinced by the bribery of pleasure and acceptance. That's definitely been the story of my life. I don't dream of nights like that often, but clearly there is something in the air in this place that just brings every single thing from my past back to the forefront. My thoughts are interrupted again when Mikayla decided I was taking too long.

"Out of bed, little lady. Time to get up."

Fine, fine. Let's do this. I get out of bed and Mikayla turns around so I can get dressed comfortably. You know, she has been such a good friend to me and has really surprisingly been helping me a lot since she's been here. I feel like I should try harder to do the same.

"So, how have you been feeling lately?" I ask as I'm getting ready. "Pretty good, actually. Whatever mediation they gave me is like a miracle candy, I freakin' love it. It's like the voices in my head are choking on the pills or something because they barely speak up anymore." I was genuinely happy to hear that from her. She deserves peace and a good friend.

"Wow, that's amazing. I'm really happy for you. And, ya know, if those voices ever start creeping back, you can always come to me and I can try to help quiet them down," I turned around towards her when I finished getting dressed. She must have felt me smiling at her, because she knew to turn around too and smiled back.

"Thanks, Tori. That means a lot! What about you? Are your medications working?" That's a very interesting question. Are they working? Or is it Mikayla that's working? Or is it both? I don't really know, to be honest.

"I think so. I think it's a combination of things. I never really had a true friend before that I felt comfortable talking so openly and honestly with. I didn't think it would help me, but maybe it has been."

Wow. I may actually be getting help in here. Me. Who would have ever thought that was possible?

"I feel the same way, Tori. And now you're stuck with me for life!" she said as she let out a huge smile.

"Sounds good to me," I said back through giggles. She rushed straight towards me and threw her hands around me. That may have been the biggest hug I've ever gotten. I hugged her back with my one good arm and smiled.

"Okay, let's get out of here before we miss breakfast."

We walk through the hallway and make our way over to the dining room. I don't know why it's called that. When I think of a dining room, I think of a fancy, elaborate, detailed room with some artwork on the walls and a big table in the middle surrounded by a bunch of nice chairs. This is definitely way more like a tiny, middle school cafeteria, with cheap looking furniture and of course boring, grey walls. Even so, everyone here refers to it as the dining room for some reason.

In the "dining room", Liv and Jessica are sitting at one table and Mike and Andrew are sitting at another. Mikayla and I walk over to the girl's table.

"Hey guys, what's for breakfast?" Mikayla asks.

"Pancakes with bacon, oatmeal, a fruit cup and orange juice," Liv lets out. "Yeah, can't you tell it's delicious?" Jessica chimes in. I look down and notice that there were only a few bites taken off of her plate. I know she asked that to imply that the food wasn't good, but maybe she was actually just saying that to use it as an excuse to not eat. Poor girl. She should eat. Her body could definitely use the nutrition. Mikayla shrugged her shoulders and headed over to the food line to grab a tray. I don't think she was thinking about what Jessica said like I was. I don't think many people think like me. You don't really think like that unless you've been in that experience before, I think.

I walked over behind Mikayla and waited for my food in line. "Hey, have you ever seen Jessica eat?" I asked Mikayla.

"Barely. I always tell her how good the meals and the snacks are. Are they that good? Of course not. They kind of suck. But she needs to eat. I can't force her though. So, I just try to help out and be there for her however I could."

Of course, she did. Mikayla's a good friend to everyone in here, not just me.

We both get our food and then head back to the girls and have a seat. I sit down across from Jessica and smile. She gives a little half-smile back, but I could tell it was a forced smile. It almost seemed like she was going to burst out into tears. I tried to give her a look that said 'It's okay, please eat, it's good for you' and I do think she understood it. I took a bite of my food and she slowly followed me. After a few times of this repeating, I look over at Mikayla and Liv and they are watching us and smiling. They continue to eat with us and we chat about nonsense. Cute boys, annoying parents, the usual teenage girl stuff. Throughout the whole time though, I'm keeping one eye on Jessica to make sure she's okay and eating.

"I'm out of juice," Mikayla says as she starts to get up.

"I'll come with you," Liv says, who then begins to get up as well. They both start walking over to the lunch line and Jessica speaks up immediately.

"Hey, thanks for helping me. I know it probably seems stupid, but it's hard," she said with a slight look on her face that was about fifty percent gratitude and fifty percent embarrassment.

"It's not stupid. I have major self-esteem issues, especially with my weight, and there are times that I have skipped meals, and even some times that I've thrown up my meals. So, I get it. And I'm here for you."

Jessica looked at me with the biggest smile on her face I've seen yet. I genuinely want to help people in this place. Clearly everyone is here for a reason and could use some help. Mikayla has made me realise just how helpful it can be to know someone is there for you. I didn't realise how helpful that could be until I met her, so if I can help anyone in here, why wouldn't I?

Just as Mikayla and Liv come back and sit down, the boys come over to our table. They waltz over and make themselves comfortable. Andrew sits by Jessica, and Mike sits down by me.

"Hey ladies. What's shakin' bacon?" Mike asks the table. Andrew looked like he wanted to say something clever or funny too but couldn't think of anything, so he just lets out a little "hi" under his breath.

It's an interesting dynamic, the Mike and Andrew friendship. The two of them are very different, besides the fact that their mental diagnoses are very similar. Mike is a tall, dark and handsome kind of guy. He seems rugged with his messy, jet black hair and dark jeans, but also like a gentleman. He's very outgoing and wants to be involved in every conversation. Andrew, on the other hand, is short and quiet.

He seems almost like a nerdy, sweet type. His brown hair always looks perfect, along with his perfectly stitched pants and polo shirts. He's shy and would much rather not be in the centre of a conversation. Mike gives Andrew confidence in here, helps him feel more comfortable around the rest of us and tries to teach him how to be "cooler" and more sociable. In exchange, Andrew helps Mike a lot with schoolwork. All of our own high schools send work here for us to do while we are here if we are up for it so we don't fall too far behind, and I've seen Andrew helping and almost tutoring Mike. The friendship seems odd and unlikely, but it works out for them.

"What's cookin', good lookin'?" I whisper under my breath, but I guess it wasn't really a whisper, because everyone seemed to hear me. Where the hell did that come from? Why did I feel so comfortable to be myself around these people? Mike laughed, which meant Andrew laughed and the girls giggled while all looking at me like they were just as shocked as I was with that response.

"Touché, Tori," Mike said with a smile. We all sat around chatting again about usual teenage stuff. After a few minutes, it seemed a little relentless.

"Let's go in the hang out room for a bit," I suggested. We all got up from the table, threw our empty food trays away and headed for the hang-out room.

"Mike, maybe you can teach Tori that video game now," Liv said.

"Yeah, and you guys can create characters who fall in love," Jessica added. Was it even that type of video game? I had no idea, and neither did she. She just wanted to throw that in there to "subtly" drop some kind of hint. Oh God, my dear friend anxiety is back. I can't handle this right now.

"On second thought, I didn't sleep so great last night. I'm really tired, I think I may just go and lay down for a little bit. I'll catch up with you guys later." Before anyone could say anything else to me, I bolted out, down the hallway and towards my room. I figured the girls knew what they did, considering it wasn't the most subtle exit I could have made, but I just couldn't deal with it in that moment. I know they didn't mean anything bad by it, but I just need a break. I go into my room, sit on my bed, and try to let the anxious moment fade away. As soon as I start to try and calm down a little bit, though, it comes right back with a simple voice.

"Hey, Tori, can we talk for a minute?" I hear from the doorway. I turn to look and see Mike standing there. What could he want to talk to me about? So much for letting the anxious fade moment.

"Hi. Um, sure," I reply in a low voice, trying to stay as calm, cool and collected as I possibly can. He walked in the room a little more and gave me a serious, yet sincere look.

"I just wanted to apologise for being a jerk the other day. I don't know what came over me. Sometimes I just can't control my feelings and my words, but I'm working on it. Sometimes, my borderline just takes over and the moods are just out control and I just…"

"It's okay. You don't have to explain." I could tell he was about to ramble and it seemed like he was getting nervous and tripping over his words, so I cut him off before he said anything else. Wow though, I wasn't really expecting that. I forgave him for what he said, but I didn't forget about it.

"It's okay Mike. Maybe you were right…"

This time, he cut me off before I could say anything else.

"No, I wasn't! See, this is why I wanted to talk to you. I was just being a jerk.

I wasn't right. It's good that you didn't do any of those other things because then there would have been a bigger chance that you wouldn't be alive today. And it's good that you're alive. You deserve to be alive."

Wow, also wasn't really expecting that either. I do think he was more right the first time though.

"What makes you say that? You barely know me." I think that came out a little meaner than I meant it to sound.

"Because. I just do. You're nice, and pretty, and smart. And I could see what you were doing for Jessica at breakfast. That was nice of you. You're a nice person, Tori. You should be able to see that."

I just looked at Mike like he said the most absurd thing ever. Honestly, I don't see that. I don't see anything positive about myself, otherwise why would all these things have happened to me? And why would I have been hurt so many times? Why would everyone leave me? Why would he leave me? Like our relationship meant nothing?

I don't know how to trust people anymore, especially guys. I don't know to take a compliment, because how do I know if he really means it or if he's just saying that for an ulterior motive? I have a lot of guys to thank for making me this way, and others for proving my point that I'm not enough for anyone.

"You look like you're about to roll your eyes at me," he says, after I didn't respond to his compliment. He's right, I definitely felt an eye roll coming on, but I was trying to stop it so I wouldn't come off as a cold-hearted brat. I think a little one might have slipped out though.

"Damn, what did he do to you?" he asked. How did he know? "What do you mean?" Just play dumb, Tori. Just play dumb.

"No girl acts like this unless they've been hurt and betrayed by a guy, she once thought was her knight in shining armour or her prince charming."

Interesting choice of words. He was definitely charming. Maybe too charming. But wow, maybe Mike wasn't as dumb as he made himself seem the other day. Maybe it really was just his borderline personality disorder getting in the way. I could understand that, my mental illness takes over me a lot too. As soon as he finished his sentence, I felt the tears build up in my eyes. God, Tori, don't cry. Do. Not. Cry. I fought with everything I had to keep myself from letting go, but he could tell I was not okay. He gave me a look that said "it's okay, I won't judge you, I'll listen" and I'm not really sure why, but I believed it. I stop fighting, just a little bit, and a few tears rolled down my cheek. The second I started crying, Mike was there. He came over and sat on my bed right next to me. I could tell that he wasn't sure if or how he should touch me to try to be comforting. Instead, he just sat there and let me cry in front of him, without any judgement. That's a new feeling for me. After about a minute or two of my tears and semi-uncomfortable silence, he spoke up.

"You can talk to me, Tori," he said to me in a very genuine voice accompanied with a soft, sweet smile. Again, I don't know why, but I believed him. I do really feel like he meant it. That he did actually care, and that I really could talk to him.

"I just feel so destroyed. Dead inside. Like I've been killed in every way but physical and now I'm left to take care of that on my own." Wow, did I really just say that out loud? I couldn't get myself to look at Mike, so I just kept looking down.

"What did he do?" Mike asked. I could tell he was still rattled by my previous response, but he tried to not show it.

"It doesn't matter what he did. How I feel about what he did is all that really matters now."

109

"And that is?"

Well, he asked for it. He wanted it, he got it. Here goes nothing.

"I feel manipulated. I was told everything I've been waiting to hear from a guy forever. He made me feel like I was special. Like I was beautiful. For once in my life, I believed I was worthy of being loved like that. For once, I had hope. Just to have it taken away from me. To feel like he didn't truly love me in the same way that I loved him and needed me like he said he did, it hurts. A part of me feels lied to. The other part feels like even if he has feelings for me, they aren't enough for us to be together. And that's just as bad in a different way. Another part of me sometimes feels that he knew all along that I was just a temporary thing for him, when the whole time, I look like the fool planning a future and really seeing a permanent, life-long relationship. He let me fall in love with him, and he became the person I've always dreamt of as a little girl, meanwhile, all along, I should've known that I was never going to be enough for him."

Wow, I feel like I just read a lengthy monologue from a romance novel or something. It actually felt amazing to say it all out loud. It felt amazing to actually tell someone. I had let out tears again, this time, a lot more, but I got myself to look at Mike. Talk about rattled. I definitely don't think he expected all of that from me. I honestly didn't expect it either. After what I noticed was a long enough silence, I realised that I had more to say and spoke up again. I'm already this deep underwater, I might as well just keep swimming.

"You know what's the saddest part about the whole thing, though? He was my friend first. He was my best friend. He knew more about me than anyone else. I gave him the power

110

to hurt me and trusted him not to, but he did. Maybe it's my fault for thinking that we were in the same place; that I meant to him what he meant to me. Maybe it's my fault for putting my guard down and actually letting myself be happy and fall in love. It was real to me; I was all in. I truly believed that he was my soulmate, in every way. I offered him my life, I gave him my whole heart, and I still wasn't enough."

Holy crap, it just kept coming, like word vomit. Without realising it, I must have stood up and got angry, because when I finished my rant, I was looking straight at Mike and breathing really heavy. Geez, calm down Tori. He still looked rattled, but also heartbroken at the same time.

"It's not your fault, Tori," he muttered. He obviously didn't know what to say, and who could blame him? I'm practically a stranger. After I finally caught my breath and gathered my brain for a second, the tears came back. I slid down the edge of my bed and planted myself on the floor.

"Why am I not enough?" I somehow muttered through my tears. Mike joined me on the floor the second the question left my lips.

"Hey, you are enough. Just because this guy isn't smart enough to see it does not mean it isn't true. It just means that there is someone better out there for you who will see it, and when they do, they will mean what they say, and they will never let you go."

Well, who knew this kid was so sensitive and caring? I would have never guessed that, especially after our first encounter and the way he carries himself and "acts" in public. But again, this is why I don't judge a book by its cover.

"Mike, I don't know how I am supposed to move on from this. I mean, I was already so broken before him, and now, I just feel completely obliterated. I honestly don't think I am capable of trusting people, especially guys. Not anymore, not after all of this."

I went to look down again, but Mike grabbed my hand and I instantly found myself turning to him, gravitating to the left to look at him.

"You are. Maybe you're not ready yet, but someday, you will be, and when you meet that person, you will be able to trust again. You'll know he's the one because the trust will come effortlessly, even after what this guy did to you. Until then, that guy, your real soulmate, will just keep on waiting for you."

As soon as he finished talking, he gave me a little smirk that actually made me giggle. I don't know if I could totally believe him yet, but I still appreciated it, especially because I could tell he truly meant it. I followed the giggle with a quiet "thank you", and he gave me the tightest hug. I wasn't expecting it, but it surprisingly felt so nice. Wait, was Mike talking about himself? For some reason, I did trust him almost instantly and effortlessly, even though he was so rude the first time we met.

Could the girls be right? Could Mike actually like me? I snapped back into reality when the hug was released. Before I knew it, Mike was standing in front of me with his arms out towards me, like he was gesturing for me to grab his hands so he can pull me up off the floor.

"So, what's this guy's name, anyway? Want me to kick his ass?" he asked with a smile. I know he was kidding, but I do wish that he could understand how what he did to me really affected me, and maybe even, just for a second, feel the hurt I feel, but I also know that's not possible because emotionally, we were in two different relationships. I smiled back at Mike and reached out with my good arm to grab his hand. He pulled me up and our faces were just inches away from each other.

Welcome back, anxiety. We stared at each other like we were both lost in a trance for a few seconds. Somehow, reality hit for the both of us at the same time and we both took a step or two back.

"So, um, I'll see you later, then?" he asked. He sounded rattled again, but it seemed like a different kind of rattled this time, more like a nervous kind of rattled.

"Sure," I let out quietly, along with a little half-smile.

"Okay, cool. See ya," he turned and walked towards the door, but suddenly stopped in the doorway and turned back around to face me.

"Tori?"

"Yeah?" Oh God, what was he going to say? Glad you're getting comfortable here, anxiety.

"That guy may have lied to you in a lot of ways, but you are special. And you are beautiful."

Like an idiot, I blushed immediately. Geez, how freaking embarrassing. He turned back around and left the room. I instantly melted onto my bed the second he was out of my line of vision. What the hell just happened? Maybe it wasn't my dear old friend, anxiety. Could it have been butterflies? Dear God, not again. I'm so not ready. And even if I thought I was, I will never be over my ex. How could I be? Especially not now. That wound is so deep and so sharp and so fresh still, there's no way I am in a good place to even think about another relationship. Yet I can't stop thinking about Mike right now! What is going on? Regardless, I have to get through this first, and completely get over him and deal with that painful love. I know that will take some time for me to do, and I know that I need to just take one thing at a time. But still, maybe it was butterflies? God, I need a nap. I need my mind to stop for a minute.

One. Two. Three. Four.
Could the girls have been right?
Five. Six. Seven. Eight.
Could Mike be right?
Nine. Ten. Eleven. Twelve.
Please let me sleep.

Chapter Nine
Night Eight – The Love Story
I'll Never Write

11:10 am

"Okay, get prepared. Think. Focus. It's that time of day again, don't let it go to waste." I watch the clock methodically, studying the narrow, minute hand as it slowly ticks. Tick. Tock. Tick. Tock.

11:11 am

"Think. Focus. Pray." I close my eyes oh so tight, and think. I think about you. I think about your body, your smile, your laugh, and what it would be like to have you. I imagine your presence, and how it would bring a smile to my face. I haven't had a genuine smile in so long, and I focus on that lost feeling. I breathe in, breathe out, and keep my eyes shut. "I wish for you." I open my eyes, and glance up at the clock; 12 seconds to spare.

11:12 am

No matter how many 11:11's it takes, I will never stop wishing for you.

11:10 pm

"Okay, second opportunity, don't let it go to waste. Think. Focus."

Again, I set my sights on the clock. The minute hand taunts me. A watched pot never boils, but if you think I am taking my eye of the time you must be crazy. This time comes twice a day, because everybody deserves a second chance. And I am ready for it. Tick. Tock. Tick. Tock.

11:11 pm

"Okay, here we go again. Think. Focus. Pray." Again, I close my eyes.

Again, I think about you. I focus on your face, and get lost in your beautiful eyes. Brown, like mine, but complimented with a slight rim of hazel. I look into your soul, and it opens up my heart to your aura. I breathe in, breathe out, and keep my eyes shut. "I wish for you." I open my eyes, and glance up at the clock; four seconds to spare.

11:12 pm

No matter how many 11:11's it takes, I will never stop wishing for you."

"Tori, it's time for your medication."

I jumped a little at the sound of a loud, unexpected voice and quickly stuff my paper and pen under my pillow. I take my medication every single night at the same exact time, you think I would be expecting it by now, yet I am still always startled by the randomness of the voice.

It's the only reason now that any hospital worker really comes in here for me anymore. I eat all of my meals out in the dining room with the group, I go to school, I go to the therapy sessions without being forced, so they don't really have any reason to come check on me anymore other than this.

"Thank you, Amy." It's always the same woman who brings me my medication. It's also the only time I ever see her working. I wonder what else she does when she's not bringing everyone their meds. She stands and watches me take my pills, like she does every night. The second I finish swallowing; she always says the same thing.

"Let me see that tongue, please."

She tries to say it in a playful way, I guess so it's not so serious and weird but it's still annoying to have to open my mouth and stick out my tongue for her. I know she's just doing her job and I'm sure there are people who hide their medication because they don't want to take them, but I am actually trying to get better.

Sometimes I don't really get medication. How do I know that it's working? It's not a miracle worker, it's not just going to fix things and make me happy, even though if you ask Mikayla, she would probably tell you the opposite. For me, though, I feel like it's hard to know if it's working. What if whatever I am feeling is situational? What if I relapse? Does that mean that the medication doesn't work at all? Or could it just work a little bit and other times, like during really difficult times, they aren't as effective? I'm not really sure how it works, but they haven't negatively impacted me up to this point, so I take them, and I would even if she wasn't watching me.

I wait a minute until I'm sure that the coast is clear and I take my pen and paper out from under my pillow. I sit on my bed with my back up against the wall and start writing again.

"Fear: a distressing emotion aroused by impending danger, evil, pain, etc., whether the threat is real or imagined.

Happiness: mental or emotional state of well-being defined by positive or pleasant emotions ranging from contentment to intense joy.

Love: a strong feeling of affection and concern toward another person, as that arising from kinship or close friendship.

How could I be feeling all of these conflicting emotions at once? Can I be scared and excited at the same time? They are such inverse feelings; how could it be possible to experience both within the same moment?

I close my eyes and I see you. I empty my mind and I think of you. Isn't that the way love should be? I've tried so hard to keep myself grounded that I've actually fallen, harder than I ever have before. And no matter how much I feel like I should get up and continue walking, I just lay there in awe of these emotions that I never thought possible in my life. And when I do try to get up, I just can't. My heart has become stronger than my body.

This is the kind of love I've been craving for so long, so why am I so afraid of it? Am I afraid of the unknown? Or am I just afraid to be happy?"

Why will I never write it? Because my love-life has only ever been filled with heartbreak and negativity. It's pathetic, really. Nobody has ever truly wanted me back, and I can't say that I blame them. I don't want me either. I mean, who would want to read about that? I don't even want to live it.

Mikayla is still in the hang-out room with everyone. I was there earlier, but came back here to write. Sometimes I need my solitude, and I just need to write and release some feelings. Obviously, I can't cut in here, but that doesn't mean I don't have the urges. They aren't as strong, maybe because of the medication, maybe because of Mikayla, I'm not sure, but they are still there. I don't think they'll ever go away, but writing helps me let out whatever I'm thinking or feeling without fear of ridicule. My journal never judges me. I think I would have a mental breakdown if I couldn't write in here.

I put my pen and paper under my bed, making sure, as always, that it's out of plain sight. I lay down, focus on my breathing, and think.

A part of me has given up on the whole love thing. The mixed emotions, the confusion, the constant worrying that the other person is just going to wake up one morning, see me the way I see myself and stop loving me. It does not seem worth the risk anymore, especially after what just happened with him. It's weird though, because then there is this other part of me, the part that still wishes for love and a happy ever after on each and every 11:11. As a kid, it always felt like falling in love was a given, like it was just so simple and so common and it was just meant for everyone. I've decided though, that for myself, love like that is not meant for me. I'd love to not give up and keep looking, but after what this last guy did to me, I'm too scared, and I don't think it's worth the risk. It's kind of like expecting the worst but hoping for the best. It's a love story that I crave, but am afraid of at the same time. I'll never write it, and I'll probably never live it either.

Chapter Ten
Day Nine – The Lunch Bunch

"That first line. That first high. There's nothing like it. She slouches over, pressing her nose gently against the surface of the endurable end table adjacent from her bed frame. Tube in hand and eyes closed, she goes in for the kill. She inhales as much air and pixie-dust as her lungs and nose allow. She leans back, eyes still closed, and rests her head against the wall, feeling its coolness quiver through her body. A few seconds later, she repeats the process.

Snort. Relax. Repeat. Snort. Relax. Repeat.

Satisfied, her head rises and she looks over to her left. She meets the gaze of her stuffed animals, almost feeling guilty by engaging in such devilish behaviour in front of their innocent selves. Knowing that her actions cannot be undone, she sits there, waiting for the high to kick in as her love of pixie-dust continues to deepen."

I suddenly wake up and my eyes meet the bumps on the ceiling, just like they do every morning. My body has a funny habit of waking up in the middle of dreams like that. Dreams that recount memories of my life, and nightmares that retell horrors I've experienced. No matter how much I try to forget these things, my mind can't seem to let them go.

Many people don't remember their dreams, but I always do. I have always had a memory like that, where things just stick, even the small things. Something tiny my ex once said to me. A quick, embarrassing moment. Little things that most people forget after a few years stick with me forever.

Amazing how something as minuscule as pixie dust can have such omnipotent power over a human being. I mean, I was never a drug addict or anything, but whatever it took to ease the mental pain for even just a little bit was worth it, ergo, my self-harm addiction. It's amazing how any addiction, really, whether it be cutting, cocaine, sex, etc. can take over someone's life like that. Just look at what cutting has done to my life. Obviously, my problems are much greater than just cutting, but it's definitely an issue and definitely a major influence as to why I am where I am now.

"Tori, are you awake yet?" I hear, whispered from my doorway. I can tell it's Mikayla by the inflection in her voice; her "whispers" were always too loud to be classified as a whisper.

"Come on, we miss you!"

Was that Jessica? I look at the clock and it says 12:19 pm. Damn, I slept all morning? I tend to do that in this place sometimes, but after yesterday, my brain was fried, and I guess really needed to rest.

"Come have lunch with us!"

And there's Liv. I should have known. Lunch is at 12:30 pm every afternoon.

"You guys go ahead; I'll meet you there." I say to them from my room. I guess I have to get out of bed sometime.

I get up and start getting dressed when I hear the girls start to walk away. I wonder what's for lunch today; hopefully something Jessica likes. I'm sure it makes it somewhat easier for her to eat when it's something she likes.

I finish getting ready and head down the hallway towards the dining room. I look in and see everyone sitting at the same table. Andrew sees me and lets out a sweet smile. He's a nice boy, just so quiet and shy. Mikayla is sitting next to him, who is obviously the exact opposite of that. She notices me next.

"Hey Tori!" she says loudly and motions for me to come in. I walk in and say hi to everyone before getting my food. I head to the counter and see the food options: a slice of pizza or a cheeseburger, mashed potatoes or French fries, salad, rice and a cookie. Sounds, looks and usually tastes like typical cafeteria food. I make a plate and head back over to the table.

"Mike, move over a little bit so Tori can sit," Jessica says. Way to be obvious, Jess. Mike slides over, and I sit down next to him.

"Hey," I say to Mike somewhat quietly.

"Hey Tori. Sleep well?" he asks with a big smile, like he was genuinely happy to see me.

"I don't know about well, but definitely a lot," I reply.

"Yeah, I get that," He replied back with a smile.

Amongst the table, everyone starts chatting. I look at Jessica and can tell that she's eating and she actually seems happy. It seems like a different person than the person I had breakfast with a few days ago. She's been doing a good job eating, I'm proud of her. I think she can see that no one judges her for eating, but that we actually want her to eat and be healthy.

My thoughts get interrupted by a soft, gentle voice. Without even seeing the person's face, I knew who it was.

"Hey guys! How are we all doing today?"

I turn around and see Dr S. behind me. She rests her hands on Mike and Liv's shoulders.

"We're good, Dr S. Just enjoying the delicious food in our fancy dining room," Mike replied, and we all let out a little giggle at his sarcasm. I guess everyone else felt the same way about the whole cafeteria vs. dining room thing as I did. Dr S. chose to ignore his sarcasm.

"Well, I'm glad for you, Mike. Enjoy it!" Either she was ignoring it or she was playing along with it, because I could hear a hint of sarcasm in her tone too. She looks over at me and smiles.

"Tori, we meet again tomorrow. Don't forget about your assignment," she says. How did she know I didn't do it yet? I didn't forget, I have just been thinking about it for a while first.

"I won't Dr S," I reply back.

She smiles and nods back to me before she begins to walk towards the door.

"Enjoy your five-star meal, kids. See you later," she says with a smile and a wink as she walks out.

"I like Dr S. She seems to be cool," Mikayla says to the table.

"Yeah, and she's very nice," Liv adds.

"I'm not really good at the whole therapy thing," Andrew says, quietly.

"Yeah, well that's probably because you never speak," Mike added, in a joking tone that made it obvious he wasn't

123

trying to be mean but that he was just messing around with him. I guess they have that brother-like relationship now.

"No. It's just weird for me," Andrew says back.

"I like it. It's kind of cool to just be able to say whatever I want," Jessica adds. "I'm the same way as you, Andrew. I'm not crazy about therapy. It's never been my thing. I'm not comfortable. I feel that it's hard for me to talk to someone on that kind of level like that when they can't relate," I say. Everyone went quiet for a second, like what I said sounded weird or wrong or something. I don't think so; to me, it makes total sense.

"Yeah, Tori, I feel the same way. I just didn't know how to word it. Another reason why therapy isn't a great fit for me. I struggle to find words sometimes," Andrew adds. I've never heard him talk this much, really, so I'm glad that he feels comfortable to talk with all of us.

"From what I've heard, Dr S has been through more than she lets on," Jessica says.

"Really?" Liv asks.

"Yeah, I've heard that too. I think depression and anxiety," Mikayla responds.

"Yeah, and I think some kind of an abusive relationship, too," Mike adds. "How do guys know that?" I ask. Where did they get this information from? "Before you hung out with us, we had a guest speaker come to one of the groups. His name was Jeff. He used to be a patient here and just talked to us about hope and determination and stuff like that. Anyway, he spoke to us individually afterwards and basically gave me the 411 about Dr S. He was a pretty cool dude," Mike replies to me.

"Oh. So, what does the S stand for?" I ask.

"Weirdly enough, that's like the one thing I don't know. Neither did Jeff," Mike says back.

"I think she gets us and can relate to us and probably even help us more than we think she can," Jessica adds.

"Yeah, I guess you're right," I reply.

See, this is why you don't judge a book by its cover. It's a very conflicting feeling, knowing that Dr S has been through similar things like me. On one hand, I feel sorry for her. I would never wish what I have been through on anyone, not even my worst nightmare. She's a nice woman, so it makes me sad that she has lived a life similar to mine. On the other hand, though, it is helpful for me to know that she can relate to some of what I talk to her about. She's more than just brains, she's heart too, and that makes me feel more comfortable talking to her; knowing that she's been through hard times in her life like me and she can actually relate on a personal level, rather than just an academic level.

Everyone finishes up their lunch and we make our way towards the hang-out room. Mike and Andrew go straight to their video game, as usual, and the girls and I sit on the couch and chat about whatever girly topic they choose.

"Do you guys want to play a board game or something?" Mikayla asks.

"Or we have cards. How about War?" Jessica adds.

"Sure, I'm in," Mikayla says as she gets up and heads over to the shelf next to us to get the cards.

"Do you guys want to play?" Jessica asks as she turns towards me and Liv. "No thanks, I'll just watch," Liv replies.

"I'm good too. Thanks," I say.

Mikayla begins dealing the deck in half as Liv nudges me. I look towards her and she makes a weird face at me, like she's

125

trying to tell me something, but I couldn't place my finger on it.

"I'll be right back. I'm going to go to the bathroom," she says as she begins to stand up. As she stands, she makes the same face as me, this time nodding her to motion to me that she wants me to follow her.

"I'll come with you; I have to go too," I add. I don't think Mikayla and Jessica really even noticed. They seemed too into their card game.

> Two, Five. Jessica wins.
> King, Eight. Mikayla wins.
> Six, Queen. Jessica wins.
> Four, Ace. Mikayla wins.
> Seems like a pretty intense game.

I get up and begin to walk towards the door of the hang-out room, but Liv isn't there. I exit to the hallway and she's still nowhere to be found. I walk down the hall, heading towards the bathroom when I hear a voice.

"Pssst. Tori. In here."

I look towards the whisper and see Liv sitting on her bed in her room. I walk in and sit down next to her.

"What's up? Is everything okay?" I ask.

"Have you… you know… done "it"… since you've been in here?" she replies with a very concerning look on her face of fear as well as anxiety. It? What does she mean?

"What do you mean, Liv?"

"You know…" she says as her eyes look down toward her arm. Oh, I know what she means now.

"You mean cut?" I ask. I knew that's what she meant, but I wonder why she wouldn't actually just say it.

"Yes," she says, eagerly.

"No, I haven't. Have you?" I ask her, trying not to sound judgmental of whatever the answer is going to be.

"No. First of all, how would I, right? And second of all, I don't really want to. I mean, don't get me wrong, I so want to, but I also don't want to because I am in here trying to get better, just like everyone else, but I still have the urges at night when I'm alone and I'm thinking and I'm sad and it's just driving me crazy."

I could tell she was beginning to ramble because she began speaking a mile a minute and she wasn't pausing to take a breath. I definitely understand everything she is saying and feeling right now.

"Liv, take a breath. First of all, you should be very proud of yourself. I know how hard it is, trust me." Before I could finish speaking, she cut me off.

"I know you do and that's why I felt like I could talk to you about it but didn't want to in front of the other girls. I also don't have my music in here or anything that I usually try first as coping mechanisms before I actually cut, you know? I feel like I'm going crazy," she adds.

"That's okay, Liv. I get it. You're not going crazy. This is all just new. Help is hard. That's why we are here; because we need help getting help to get better," I said, really trying hard to comfort her.

This is what I meant about addictions; they will drive people nuts. I still get the urges too, so I understand exactly what she is going through. Poor thing. I genuinely care about the girl and want to help her if I can.

127

"I know you do. Thank you. It's helpful just to know that you're here if I really feel like I am going to lose it," she says as she finally lets out a breath. I'm glad she feels comfortable talking to me.

"Do you have an urge right now?" I ask, again, being very aware of my tone. I know how people have asked me things like this before, and there is a difference between sounding caring and sounding curious.

"Kind of, but I don't know why! Nothing happened, there was no real 'trigger' or anything. One second I was okay, the next I was thinking about it and not okay," she says. I guess this kind of random urge doesn't happen to her often. I, on the other hand, get these all the time, just from thinking about everything. I've always been an overthinker, and that tends to be enough to push me there.

"That's okay, Liv. You don't have to always know why you get an urge. I get them randomly all the time, just by thinking about all of that crap that either happened to me or that is going on now. What matters though is how we handle it."

A part of me feels like a hypocrite for trying to give her advice and keep her from cutting. I have the same problem, but I have a hard time taking my own advice. I've always been good at helping people, that I know, but when it comes to me, I can't help myself. I've always been more of a 'do what I say and not what I do' kind of person. Is that being hypocritical? I hope not. I'm just trying to help.

"How about this? Obviously, cutting in here seems impossible, which is probably a good thing for us right now. When we get out of here, obviously, it will be harder because there will be more temptation and more means to do it. So, we have to practice our coping mechanisms now so we can be more prepared when we leave here. When you feel an urge, you come to me. When I feel an urge, I come to you. We'll just sit and talk about it, or, we can do something to distract ourselves from it and let it try to pass."

Wow, I kind of sounded like a therapist right there for a second. I bet Dr S would be proud.

"Thank you, Tori. You're a really good friend," she said with a smile. "You're welcome," I replied back with a smile of my own. I could tell she was starting to calm down and was definitely back to breathing normally. After about a minute or so, I chimed in again.

"Are you ready to go back in the hang-out room?" I ask. After a few deep breaths, she responds back.

"Yeah, I'm ready. Let's go," she replies. We both get up off of her bed, exit her room and walk down the hallway backs towards the hang-out room.

"It's war-time, baby!" I hear Mikayla shout. Liv and I walk in and head over to them to watch the rest of the game.

Two threes.

One card, two cards, three cards, flip.

Seven, Ten. Mikayla wins.

"Yes! Come to mama, cards," she says as she reaches out and grabs the pile of cards in front of her.

"Damn," Jessica says as she rolls her eyes. During her eye roll, she must have noticed me and Liv.

"Hey, where did you guys go?" she asked. I guess they didn't hear us.

"Just for a walk," Liv answered quickly.

"Who's winning?" I ask.

"Mikayla, but I think she may be cheating," Jessica whispered, but in a joking way that was meant to be loud enough for Mikayla to hear.

"Hey, I heard that! No, I'm not, you're just a sore loser," Mikayla replied back, also in a joking way.

"Let's start over. Come on, you guys have to play this time," Jessica pleads to Liv and I.

"Okay, let's play," Liv said.

"Alright, deal us in," I agreed.

Mikayla takes the deck of cards, shuffles them all together and then starts dealing them to split the deck evenly four ways.

"Did you guys know that card games were the most common pastime for soldiers while they were away at war? While they were waiting in trenches, hospitals and war strategy rooms," she asks us as she's dealing. We all nodded with looks on our face that said "interesting, but let's just play". She must have been a good student, because she's very smart, and clearly loves history.

Mikayla brought up an interesting point though. If you think about it, we're soldiers too, just in a different war. It's ironic, really; each of us is fighting our own personal, internal war with ourselves. We go into battle, guns blazing, every day, just like our soldiers overseas, and just like these cards every hand. Gotta love irony.

Chapter Eleven
Night Nine - Dear You

"I sit at my desk with pen and paper in my hand, waiting for the words to come to me. There are so many of them, all jumbled around in my head, but getting them on paper to say what I need to say seems extraordinarily difficult. Will I ever show this to you? Probably not. How could I? But a girl could dream, that you could possibly even begin to understand the pain you are putting me through. After staring down at a blank piece of paper for what feels like forever. I finally begin:

"Dear You,

The concept of time is a complex one that's always left me dumbfounded. They say that time heals all wounds, but if anything, wouldn't that make for a larger duration for the pain to linger?

It's been almost six months, and, honestly, the time hasn't changed shit. You look like Heaven, while I feel like Hell. When I look at you, all I see are the crippling memories that lurk around my shadow and taunt me. You no longer simply cross my mind, but you now live there; you eat, sleep, breathe, and vacation there. I can't seem to remember to forget you. I do tend to forget things easily; maybe I'll try forgetting to remember you next time.

Maybe then my mind can live in peace. I thought you would always be my everything, but now, as I sit here and write you this letter that you'll never receive, I realise that I am nothing. At this moment, I realise that I will never be your anything again. And that leaves me more dumbfounded than the concept of time.

Sincerely Yours,
Me."

My eyes suddenly open and I'm left looking at the popcorn ceiling above me with a heavy heart. I wish I could get him to understand what he has to done to me. I am trying to move on, but I feel without some kind of closure, I will never be able to fully accept what he has done to me and begin to move on from it.

I look over at the clock and it reads 4:01 am. Suddenly I'm reminded by this coincidental nightmare that I have therapy with Dr S. in about six or seven hours and I haven't done my assignment yet. I look over and see that Mikayla is sound asleep. She actually looks like she's smiling. At least one of us is having good dreams. I guess there is no time like the present, right? Not like I'm going back to sleep any time soon.

I turn on the small table lamp that sits on the nightstand next to my bed and pull out my pen and paper from underneath it. Just like in the dream, I sit and stare at the blank piece of paper, not really even knowing where to start. Suddenly I'm hit with a huge déjà vu moment. Writing a suicide note is something I can do; Lord knows I wrote a million of them in my head. But writing THE suicide note? That's tough. It was difficult enough for me to write my real one, and now I have to write three, and they all have to be in clear, cut, open, honest, words. One to me, one to my parents, and one to someone of my choosing. Who am I going to write it?

Okay Tori, think. Start with the easiest one. Writing to myself shouldn't be too hard. Okay, here we go. I take a deep breath and begin to write, and wouldn't you know it, as I soon I start, it just seems to flow.

Dear Me,

Who do you think you are? You're nothing special. There are way more people out there skinnier than you, prettier than you, smarter than you, and just overall better than you. You're disgusting, and worthless, and you are not now, and never will be, good enough for anyone. You can't blame anyone for not wanting you. I don't even want you. All you do is cause pain and sadness for others. It would be better for a lot of people if you would just die already. Nobody is ever going to truly love you the way you want them too – how could they? You will never be anyone's first choice, in any way. You can offer your whole world, your whole life to someone, and they will reject it because you will never be enough. Look at what has been done to you. Look at what HE did to you. Him, of all people. There is no need for hope anymore; there is no point. It's time to do what needs to be done and just end it all, for the sake of yourself, and for others. You know there is nothing for you to truly hold on to for true happiness here, so what's the point? Everyone will make it through. Even if they can't see it right now, you not being here is what's best for many people, including yourself. It's time to do the right thing for yourself and the rest of the world. You disgust me, and everything that's happened to you is your fault. I hate you.

Always,
Tori.

Wow, that's depressing as hell. I can't help that I hate myself, though. Look at the shit I've been through, who wouldn't hate themselves? I mean, I've been through so much shit, way more than most people go through all-in-one lifetime, so there has to be one defining factor and reason as to why: me. So yeah, I hate myself, but that's neither here or there right now.

Okay, next: Mom and Dad. Thank God they'll never be able to read this, because the note I wrote to myself was bad, but that's all stuff I already knew. This note would be destroying my parents by telling them the truth about how I really feel on this Earth, which is nothing a parent wants to hear about his or her child.

Weirdly enough, like the first one, once I started, the jumbled words in my head seemed to organise themselves as they flowed through the pen.

Dear Mom and Dad,

I'm sorry. I know that this is going to devastate you. I am not intentionally trying to hurt you, but I am in so much pain here on Earth, and I can't handle it anymore. I've been thinking for a long time about how to tell you this, but there are no words. I have finally accepted that this life just isn't for me. I wish there was another way I could be truly happy, but sadly, there isn't. Trust me, I've tried. I've tried so hard and it's just not possible. It's not what's meant for me, and I am okay with that. I promise you; you will get through this. I will always be with you to make sure of it. Try to think of it this way; your baby girl will no longer be hurting. She'll be free; free of the constant pain and sadness.

And hopefully, she will finally be happy.

I am so thankful for everything you have given me, most importantly, the love and support. You have always been my biggest fans, and I am forever grateful. Please don't ever think that any of this is your fault. You've been the best parents and friends I could have ever asked for. I love you both so much, please don't think that this means I don't. This is just something I have to do. Please don't worry about me; I will be okay, and I will finally be at peace, and I'll get to see Pop again.

Again, this is just something I need to do. Keep yourself surrounded by everyone else who will be hurting. Please relay this message to them: Do what I couldn't. Stay strong. Be kind to one another, and never give up. You all got this.

Always,
Tori.

My poor parents. I can't imagine what they must be going through with all of this. I wish I didn't put them through so much pain, they don't deserve it, and they definitely deserve a better daughter than me.

I put both notes under my pillow and began to think about who to write the last one to. Dr S said it can be someone who is very important to me. I can definitely think of a few. She also said that it can be someone who has maybe contributed to my depression and issues. I can definitely think of more than a few, but I'm not a 'Thirteen Reasons Why' kind of girl in the sense that I don't like to put blame on people. Do the people who have treated me like crap deserve to know what they've done? Yes, they do. However, I feel that once I was gone, they know deep down that they had something to do with it. And to be honest, life happens. People suck and we all know that, but nobody would be forcing me to kill myself except me. But again, that is all neither here nor there considering this letter will not be read by anyone. Now that I think about it, maybe this is what I need; maybe this is my closure. Write the note and never deliver it – he'll never know and I may feel better getting it all out and writing it towards him. This one might not be too hard after all.

Well, here we are. I've said it before, but it takes on an entirely new meaning now. The rivers aren't just running blood anymore, they are overflowing. The sky isn't just falling anymore, it's crashing. And the world is not just ending anymore: it is over.

When I was a little girl, I used to wonder about what my life would eventually turn out like. Would I have friends? Would I still be living in Port Chester? Would I have a job that I loved? Most importantly, would I ever find someone out there who fell in love with me? I prayed every night to God to someday, please send me a soulmate. Please, just let there be someone out there who will love me for me. Who will choose me first before anyone else? Who would be my other half? As a little girl, never did I think my life would be here: depressed, alone, completely heartbroken, and now a suicide attempt survivor.

For a while now, I've been going to any extreme to distract myself from thinking. Anything to disconnect and detach myself from reality, because it's all just too much for me to handle. After everything I've been through, I put my guard up. I told myself that I would never allow myself to love again. That I would never trust again. Then came along you, and I couldn't fight the feelings. I trusted you wholeheartedly in a way I never have before, and in a way, I didn't think I was or ever would be capable of. I mean, it was YOU. How could YOU ever do anything to hurt me? It didn't seem possible. For the first time since I was a little girl, I actually had hope. Hope that we would someday be together. Hope that God actually might have answered my prayers. But then that hope was shattered, and I realised I was wrong.

I had hope of true happiness and true love for once in my life dangled in front of my face and snatched away from me like a cruel, sick joke. It was so close for me to just reach out and grab it, and right when I was about to, it was taken away from me.

There is a part of me that can't blame you for leaving. I know I'm not the prettiest. I know I'm not the smartest, or the skinniest, or the easiest to be with, but what I also know is that I loved you so much, I can't even believe that it was possible for me to feel that way. I didn't know I was capable of loving someone the way I loved you. The other part of me knows that that indescribable love that I had for you would make me the best partner that you could ever have. No one would ever love you or treat you like I would. I have been so blinded by this extraordinary, unbelievable, earth-shattering love that I couldn't see the truth that was staring me in the face: it wasn't meant to be like I had thought.

Truthfully, I don't think you really believe how much this whole situation has affected me and will continue to affect me. Maybe that's because you don't want to accept it. Maybe it's because you don't fully understand how much I loved you. Honestly, I can't imagine ever being truly over you.

I hope that you never forget about this. Never forget about me.

Never forget about both the amazing times we had together and also the sad and painful nights full of blood and tears I've had on my own. I hope you never forget about any of this, because I sure won't. Everything about it hurts. How much hope I had. How close we were. And how much love and pain I'm capable of feeling.

So, the rivers are overflowing with blood, the sky is crashing down onto me, and the world has been obliterated into a million pieces, like my heart. And I'm done existing in the madness and chaos of it all.

Damn. That was intense. But also, so exhilarating. That was definitely the easiest to write, by far. I have so much to say to him, that honestly doesn't even scratch the surface, but I have to accept that it is what it is and that nothing I say to him is really going to make any kind of a difference. I have to say, it felt amazing to get that all out, kind of like when I vented to Mike. I didn't expect it to be this helpful. I also didn't expect to feel as good afterwards, like a lot of weight just lifted off of my shoulders. Hopefully, this is a good start to moving on.

Dr S is honestly going to love reading these notes, and I actually feel okay talking about this stuff now that the hardest things to say are written down on paper. She's going to love this.

I look up at the clock and it says 6:09 am. Wow, that took me two hours? I guess that's not a long time when you think about how much I had to write, and the content I had to write. It takes time, but still, it didn't feel like two hours. I put my paper under my pillow, turn off the lamp and slouch back under the covers. I look over and see Mikayla, still sound asleep, and then I look up at the popcorn ceiling and begin counting.

One, two, three, four.

I think Dr S may really know what she's talking about. Writing those notes did actually seem to help in some way.

Five, six, seven, eight.

Reading it on paper rather than just thinking it in my head seemed to open my eyes a little bit more to certain things.

Nine, ten, eleven, twelve.

It should be an interesting conversation with Dr S tomorrow. Thirteen, fourteen, fifteen, sixteen.

Maybe I can actually get a few hours of good sleep.

Chapter Twelve
Day Ten – Hello
Again, Sweetheart

People always say that everything happens for a reason. If that's true, then what's the reasoning behind war and world hunger? What about sadness or death? If the reasoning behind negative aspects of life is just strength, well that's fine, but sometimes figuring out the reasoning behind something can take too long. Some people unfortunately give in before they can find that strength in themselves. Here's another one: what doesn't kill you makes you stronger. What doesn't kill you won't always make you stronger; what doesn't kill you makes you draw on yourself with sharp objects while sobbing in the corner of your bathroom. What doesn't kill you makes you wish it had.

Another statement I hear constantly: time heals anything. I never understood that theory. For me, time just makes it worse. More time to think about everything that went wrong once upon a time. Just because time goes on doesn't mean you miss your ex-boyfriend any less or the hurt you felt isn't as painful. Time stops for no one and that could be a difficult realisation for some people. Time can be a puzzling concept to comprehend and analyse. There are moments when time is going by so fast that it leaves your mind with doubt and your heart with wonder. Other moments don't seem to be moving at all; it feels like the clock hasn't ticked in days and you're just stuck in that one aspect of time and life for eternity. Those kinds of moments are more my speed. I've been going at the same, non-moving rate since seventh grade. My self-esteem, my outlook on life, and my general emotions have been the same since it started. It's been more than half of my life now and the tears still come the same for the same reasons. I've been depressed longer than I haven't been; it's crazy. Being stuck like this, it's more surviving than it is living, really. I feel homesick from a place that doesn't exist; it's like drowning except you can see everyone around you breathing. I know I need help, and I'm trying.

What's the reasoning for all of this to be happening to me though?

Everything I have been through has to be for a reason, but I can't figure out what it is nor do I know if it's a good reason? Did it all happen because I did something wrong in a past life? Not only me, but what about the reason for things happening to Mikayla? And Liv? And Mike? And everyone else who goes through such bullshit in life. It doesn't seem to make sense, and I don't think it ever will.

My random thoughts are interrupted by a deep, masculine voice coming from my doorway.

"Tori, time for one-on-one."

I look up at the clock and it says 9:16 am. Fourteen minutes, that's more than enough time to get ready in this place. I get out of bed and change into leggings and a sweatshirt, which is basically the same kind of outfit I slept in. I give my hair a quick brushing and throw on some slippers. Eight minutes left to spare. I walk to the restroom down the hall to brush my teeth. Four minutes to spare. Not too shabby.

Down the hall I go, and boom, right on time.

I'm back in the boring white-walled, beige-carpeted office again. It looks just like I left it the first time. It almost looks too similar. Too perfect, as if no one else has been in here since my session. We know that's not true though. Hello, it's Ward C. C stands for Crazy apparently, remember?

"Hey there, Tori," Dr S. says with a smile as she enters the room. "How we doin' today?"

"I'm okay," I respond.

"Could you be more vague?" she asks sarcastically, like Chandler Bing does in the television show Friends. God, I love that show. I miss something so simple as watching whatever I want on TV, whenever I want.

"I could've said nothing and just shrugged my shoulders," I said back with a little half smile.

"Good point. Let's get started."

She sits down across from me and looks at me. I knew she was waiting for me to begin the session and to see if I was going to let her read the notes I wrote. As anxious as I'm feeling about it, I do want to get help. I am willing to put in the work to get better, and more often than not, that work is going to include anxiety for me. I hand her the notes and she gives them a quick glance over.

"Where should we start?" she asks, but before I could make a suggestion, she speaks up again.

"Dear Me…" she reads aloud, but continues to read the rest to herself.

142

When she finishes a minute or so later, she looks up at me with a sad, concerned look on her face.

"Wow, that's intense. How long do you remember feeling this way about yourself?" she asks.

"I've always felt not good enough and just like there is always someone better than me who someone else would choose over me, in any regard, and everything that has happened to me and continues to happen to me just enforces and strengthens that belief," I respond to her.

"I get that," she says. That's it? Fifteen seconds or so go by, and I decide to speak up again.

"I obviously don't want to feel this way about myself and hate myself like this. I want to be happy and like who I am, but it doesn't seem at all possible," I say in a raised voice, not realising it was so raised and I was getting so worked up over it.

"Well, that's good to hear. It sounds like you mean it, Tori."

"I do. I really do."

"Good. Then we'll continue to work on it until you get there. Once you have some sort of positive feelings towards yourself, a lot can change. Trust me," she says with a smile, and then continues on to the next note. Up next, Dear Mom and Dad. This one is a little longer, so it takes her a few minutes to read it. She finishes, and looks up at me again, this time with a serious look on her face.

"I'm going to ask you a question, and I want you to answer honestly. There will be no judgment or repercussion for your answer," she says, and I nod. Hello again, anxiety, my dear friend. I do believe her though.

"Do you still actively want to kill yourself?" she asks.

"No," I answer after a few seconds. I thought maybe she'd smile or something, but her straight facial expression did not change at all.

"And why is that? What's changed?" she asks, still blank like a piece of copy paper across her face.

"I mean, I still feel hopeless and helpless. I still hate myself, and my self-esteem is probably always going to be this low, if not get lower. I still don't think I have a happy life ahead of me. That's not just going to go away, you know, but after surviving my last suicide attempt and seeing what it did to my parents, I feel like I can't do that to them. I don't see how I can put them through that."

"So, in a way, you're saying that you are living for them, not for yourself?"

"That's exactly what I'm saying. I do not think suicide is a selfish act, but it's hard to be that person to put these two amazing people, who I love and who love me so much, through something like that again. When I woke up in the hospital and they were there, I can't explain the looks on their faces. They were angry, of course, but underneath that it was fear. Fear for a girl they love so incredibly much. I can't imagine what their faces would have looked like if I died, nor do I want to. As miserable as I may be being alive, I can't do that to them," I ramble on with as much conviction as I could. I wanted her to believe me and understand.

After I finish speaking, my body is shaking and my heart is racing, out of passion, I guess. I begin to try and calm myself down and focus on my breathing when Dr S. chimes in.

"You know sweetheart, this may sound crazy, but that's okay for now. It's okay to live for other people until you can live for yourself. Is it the healthiest way to live? No. But you'll get to a point where you will want to live for yourself. We'll get there together, but until that happens, as long as living for someone else is keeping you alive, then it's okay."

I don't know if I was totally expecting that answer, but I'm glad that's what I got. I didn't really know what to say next, so I just waited for her to speak up whenever she was ready.

"Anything else you'd like to say about that one?" she asks, as I look down with tears in my eyes. I don't know where the tears came from, really.

"What's going on?" she asks when she notices that I'm crying.

"I don't know. My parents just mean so much to me and hurting them and thinking about the hurt I put them through and the more hurt I could have put them through, it just gets to me," I respond through tears.

"Can we move on now?" I ask, wiping them from my face and trying to pull myself together to keep going.

"Of course," she says, as she begins to read the final note. This one is definitely the longest, so it took her a good six or seven minutes to get through it.

She looks up at me, yet again, but this time, with a different look on her face than I was expecting. She looked at me with a small side smile and let out a little chuckle. "Damn, you go girl." That was not the reaction I was expecting, but it made me giggle back. Did I laugh out of nervousness? It wasn't funny, but feeling validated by her did make me happy.

"This guy really hurt you, huh?" she asked, very sincerely.

"You have no idea," I say back, looking down at the ground, trying to control the tears yet again.

"The rivers aren't just running blood anymore, they are overflowing. The sky isn't just falling anymore, it's crashing. And the world is not just ending anymore: it is over."

"That's deep," she says.

"Yeah. That's how it feels inside my heart sometimes. Like it's imploding inside of me and there's nothing I can do about it," I answered immediately. No thought about it needed.

"Wow. I notice though that you used the past tense. You *loved* him. So, you don't love him anymore?"

"I do. I think I always will. It's just different right now."

"Go on," she said. I don't know how I am going to explain this and not sound ridiculous.

"It's complicated. I've never been an angry person, but sometimes, I feel so angry about this that I am just going to lose it."

"Heartbreak is an overwhelming experience of different kinds of emotions, and anger is definitely a part of it."

"Even if what we had wasn't real to him, it was real to me. He truly was everything to me, even though I wasn't everything to him. I'll always have some kind of love for him, despite what he did to me, but he cut so deep, in so many ways, so many times, sometimes I don't understand why or how I can still love him. It's confusing, and it doesn't erase the memories or the pain, and it doesn't mend the heart he obliterated or the hope he destroyed," I say, now with a tear or two falling down my cheek. I look up at her when I finish speaking, and now she's giving me that sad look again from before. She looks like she doesn't know what to say, so I speak up.

"I know, I sound crazy. He hurt me so incredibly bad, why do I still have any sort of love for him? I don't know," I say as I look back down at the ground.

"Love is complicated. Every kind of love. It's not as clear cut as 'this person hurt me so I hate them'. That's what might make sense to someone outside of our situation, and that's what might make sense to us in our brains, but our hearts work differently. Sometimes it takes some time for your heart to catch up with your head. It's not crazy that you still have feelings for this guy that hurt you so badly. That's you loving the person he was before he hurt so many times. That's you wanting what he did to you to be a misunderstanding. That's you fighting for your relationship.

The truth is, the person you loved before he hurt you didn't exist, it wasn't a misunderstanding, and he's not fighting for you like you are for him. All of it is a very hard pill to swallow, and you are absolutely entitled to your feelings and they are valid."

At this point I'm full-on crying. Dr S. notices and hands me a few tissues. "You also say in the note that he had destroyed your hope," she says as I look up to meet her gaze through tears.

"Is he the reason you tried to kill yourself?" she asked.

"No. That was my choice, and that's nothing something I would put on someone. So many things have happened, that was just another catalyst. The icing on the cake. Like everything else, it proved my point that I'm not good enough, and I didn't want to stay alive and continue to be proved right," I say back, very easily, surprisingly.

"How do you know you'll continue to be proved right?" she asks.

"Look at the past. Look at everything that's happened, and where I am now. I've been proven right enough times," I answer.

"You may think you know what's going to happen, but you truly don't. No one does. You'll be proved wrong someday. You just said that you're living for other people, and like I said, that's okay for now, but one day, when you are proved wrong and you see how amazing life can be, that's when you'll start living for yourself. So, you may not want to be here right now. You may only be here for other people, but someday, it'll be for you, and you will be so happy you survived all of this," she said with a nod and a smile. I'm glad she has so much confidence in that statement. I can only pray that she's right. The tears stopped falling, and I nod back at her with a little side smile, showing her that we are on the same page and I'm ready for some good in this life.

"So how did you feel after writing these notes?"

"I almost felt some sort of relief," I answer, wiping my face of the excess tears from before.

"Can you explain that a little more?"

"Just like these giant weights I was holding inside of me just lifted out of my soul. Seeing them as a tangible thing in my hand made them more real, but I think it's going to help me let go of those feelings."

"I think you're right. You're a writer, and I can see why. I can see why you love it. I can see why it's your outlet. Not to mention, you definitely have a way with words and the written language," she says to me. I smile back and nod as a sign of a thank you, and she lets out a smile herself.

"Really good session today, Tori. I'm proud of you. You did great," she says as the smile across her face gets bigger and bigger with every word. I look at the clock, and our session is pretty much over. It went by so fast; I couldn't believe that. I say thank you with a smile, get up and head over to the door. As I go to open it, Dr S. stops me.

"Tori?" I turned around to look at her. "You should be proud of yourself too."

"I am, actually. For the first time in my life, I am."

"I'm glad, sweetheart. See you later," she says with a smile. I head out the door, back down the hallway, and I'm smiling too. I never thought I'd leave a therapy session with a smile, but I guess anything is possible. I almost feel rejuvenated by that session with Dr S., like I can do anything. Like the world is my oyster. Like finally, for once, help is possible. I'm ready for a change. I've always been ready to feel better, but it never seemed even remotely possible. I feel ready and capable, for the first time. Maybe I don't have to feel like this for the rest of my life. Like maybe life can get better. It seems crazy that I could even think that because my life since seventh grade, for as long as I can remember, has been me feeling and being this way. Who knows, maybe I can get better? Maybe I don't have to hate myself like this forever? Oddly enough, that's a scary feeling for me, but it's also kind of like a whole new world has opened up in front of me, and Dr S is opening the door to it and telling me it's time to start over. I almost feel like a new person walking out of that room today. Damn, Dr S. is better at her job that I thought.

Chapter Thirteen
Night Ten – The Novel
I'll Never Write

I sat at the dusty bar waiting for my drink. I'm a simple girl. A Jack and Coke would suffice. To my left was an older gentleman in a trench coat and ripped jeans. You could tell from his breath as well as the four empty Corona bottles around him that he was about three sheets to the wind. I nicknamed him Corona. I chose to glance back at my drink as he started to go to work on number five.

My drink was nearly empty, but not as empty as I was feeling. I was as alone and unloved as ever, and without him, I felt like nothing. Our first kiss played over and over again in my head. Like the whiskey I was sipping on, I savoured every taste of that first kiss. And God did you taste delicious. What I wouldn't give for another sip.

I chugged the last of my drink and ordered my second one within the same minute. A few seconds later, I heard the steps of eight-inch heels walking towards me. The lady wearing them grabbed the seat directly to my right and ordered her drink, a glass of Caymus. Red wine? Who orders that in this kind of dive bar? I nicknamed her Stiletto Lady. Her little black dress was classy yet sensual and her hair was perfectly in place. Out of the corner of my eye, I saw her turn to face me. I buried my face into my drink and took a big gulp, hoping she didn't catch me analysing her.

"Something got ya down, sweetie?" Crap, she caught me.

"I'm fine, thanks though." The last thing I wanted was to be dragged into a conversation about my pathetic, problematic and no longer existent love life.

"Come on sugar, what's wrong?" Dammit. Looks I don't have a choice. "Just a guy, that's all."

"I'll stop ya right there darlin'. If a guy has been playing with your heart and fuckin' you over, you cannot give him the power to affect your happiness like this."

She was not the kind of person I expected to use the F word. After I didn't respond to her comment, she went on.

"If a guy is gonna treat ya like crap, then he is crap. Every woman should be treated like this fine wine of mine. Like most men appreciates their wine, they should appreciate their woman. The taste of wine is gently beautiful while being extremely powerful, as is a woman. Fine wine and women are so alike, why shouldn't they be treated the same?

Wine is handled so delicate when as fine as this! A woman should be too, dont'cha think?

Needing a minute to develop a reaction, I looked over to my left to check on Corona. He was face-down on the bar, snoring as loud as a car engine. I guess that seventh beer really got to him. I turned back around to respond to Stiletto Lady, but when I did, she was gone. I looked around the bar for her, but she wasn't there. A little dazed, I faced forward and looked down at my third empty drink. I stared into the glass as I heard a voice above me.

"Another round, ma'am?"

Lost in my thoughts, I pause for second, but finally I answer. "Actually, I think I'll take a glass of your finest wine please."

So why will I never write it? Because who am I, that someone would choose to read a book written by? I've only experienced pain in my life, so that's what I would write about. I'm not sure who would choose to spend their money and time to read about my pain. I don't even want to live it.

Just as I am putting my pen and paper under my pillow, one of the nurses shows up in my doorway.

"Tori, there's a phone call for you." I'm stunned. I've never gotten a phone call here before.

"Do you know who it is?" I asked. If it was my mom or dad, the nurse would have just said that like I've heard her do in the past.

"He said his name is Officer Jeffries."

An officer? Uh oh. I jump off my bed and head towards the hallway. Why would an officer be calling me? Like a police officer? Confused and a little concerned, I pick up the phone.

"Hello?"

"Hi, Tori?"

"Do I know you?"

"My name is Officer Jeffries. You probably don't remember me, but I'm the police officer who arrived first to the scene of your car accident." My jaw dropped. That was literally the last thing I would have ever expected to hear. I guess I was rendered speechless for a bit, because when I didn't know what to say to him, he spoke again.

"I looked up the phone number to the address that was on your license, and spoke to your mom. She told me that it was alright to call you and gave me this number. I hope that's okay."

I almost felt like I couldn't speak. Like I was trying to speak but couldn't physically get any words out. All I could do was nod.

"Hello, Tori, are you there?" he asked. That seemed to snap me back into reality. Duh, of course he couldn't see my nod through the phone.

"Yes, I'm here. It's okay that you called. Can I ask why you're calling though?" What could he possibly need to talk to me about?

"I don't mean to startle to you, but when I found out that you survived that accident and are walking and recovering, I just wanted to hear it for myself. You're a miracle job, Tori," he said, with a little bit of a crack in his voice. I could tell that he wasn't sure if I was okay hearing this.

"What do you mean by 'miracle job'?" I asked.

"Are you comfortable hearing about your accident? I don't want to hinder your state of mind regarding the situation." He had a point. Do I want to hear the details that I either forgot about or was unconscious during? I may never get another chance to hear about it from someone who saw it.

"Yes, I am. I'd like to know," I said quietly, pulling the cord of the phone down as I sat on the hallway floor against the wall.

"When I got to the scene, there was a bunch of smoke coming from the front of your car. The windshield was completely cracked from your head banging against it. I walked up to the car, but all I could see was black smoke, white airbags and red blood. When the ambulance came a few minutes later, I went to open the door, but it was jammed or caught on something, I think it was the seatbelt. After a few tries and a helping hand from one of the EMT's, the door finally opened and there you were," He suddenly stopped speaking, like he was getting choked up or something. I chimed in.

"What did I look like?"

"You looked dead. Covered in blood and propped up against the air bag.

Completely lifeless. I went to check your pulse, and to my surprise, I felt one. It was faint and extremely low, but it was there. When I looked at the car, I was sure that anyone involved in that accident died on impact. I got the EMT's immediately to get you out of there, and that was it. They took you out slowly and carefully to avoid causing any additional harm or damage to your body and took you to the hospital."

I shed a tear, but I'm not really sure why. I think that just picturing and trying to comprehend what he saw was really hard. Not because it was me in the accident, but because of what I put him through seeing and experiencing. I'm sure he's seen and been through worse, but still, I could hear in his voice how traumatic it was for him. I guess I didn't say anything for a while, because he spoke up again.

"You should also know that I found your suicide note. It was torn from the crash and discoloured from the smoke, but I did find it." Well, that explains why no one saw it, because Officer Jeffries had it.

"What did you do with it?" I asked.

"If you had died, I would have given it over to evidence, of course. But I found it after I felt your pulse and you were

154

already on your way to the hospital. So, I held onto it. I was going to come see you in the hospital and talk to you about it, but when I called the hospital and they told me that you were on suicide watch, I knew you were being taken care of, physically and mentally. So, I just held onto it until I could speak to you," he said.

"You still, have it?" I asked, shocked that he would have kept it.

"You are my miracle job, Tori. Nobody should have been able to survive that accident. You are one strong girl, and you may not like it, but you did survive, and you didn't die for a reason. You need to be on the Earth for a reason you don't know about yet, but you have a bigger purpose here. I hope you are learning that and realising just how much life has to offer. Yes, I kept the note, so that someday, when you are doing amazing things in this life and for this world, you can look back on it and truly see both how strong you are and how far you've come."

Wow, I was not expecting a monologue like that from a man I really don't even know, but that was one of the nicest and most heartfelt things anyone's ever said to me. I cried some more, and again, I'm not really sure why. I think the whole conversation was just emotional for me. After a few tears, I responded.

"I'm really glad you reached out to me, Officer Jeffries," I said with a smile, not that he could see, obviously, but I could just feel him smiling back at me through the phone.

"I'm glad too. Maybe when you get settled back home, I can come over sometime to your parent's house and we can talk more," he offered.

"Sure, that sounds good," I responded back.

"You're a strong girl, Tori. One of the toughest people I know. Never forget that," he said. I say thank you, we say our goodbyes and I head back towards my room. It's astounding to me that this man who doesn't even know me is so invested in my life. He put in a lot of effort to track me down, make sure I was okay, and most of all, make sure I knew just how strong and important I am. All from a man who has never even heard my voice until today. It's amazing such an unexpected person could make you feel so deeply. I'm glad he reached out, and that through such deep darkness, he focused on the light, and is trying to help me do the same.

He never even met me, but through this, knows more about me than most people. I like Officer Jeffries; I'm looking forward to talking to him again and actually meeting him for real sometime soon.

Chapter Fourteen
Day Eleven – Fresh
Air Feels Weird

"*At a desk I don't recognise, I sit still. There is a pen and a pad in front of me, and words written on the pad. Remaining still, my eyes flick down to read the note:*

If I'm still here tomorrow

I will tell you that I love you
I will tell you all the times I've thought of you
And all of the times I've prayed for you to show up at my doorstep
And choose me.

If I'm still here tomorrow
I will tell you about my dreams
Where you come to rescue me like Superman
And sweep me off my feet, up in the sky, and we fly away together
And you chose me.

If I'm still here tomorrow
I will tell you my deepest secrets
Like that naughty dreams I had sometimes
And how I knew I was in love with you after the first day we hung
out
And how much it kills to not be chosen.

If I'm not still here tomorrow
Know I love you, and know about my dreams, and about my
deepest secrets
I'm glad that I told you, so please don't forget
Because today very well may be
My last tomorrow."

I look at the note in awe, and suddenly, I vanish, with nothing left in sight but the black ink on the lined, yellow pad.

My eyes open and I'm left with nothing but the sight of the popcorn ceiling about me. Quickly I jump up, grab my pen and paper from under my pillow and start rewriting the note from the dreams. I've always been able to vividly remember my dreams for quite some time after I have them, but I didn't want to take any chances. I wanted that note written verbatim, and I knew I had it for at least a few minutes, just enough time to get it all down.

Why would I dream that? It must be because of the suicide note activity from yesterday with Dr S. I look over to tell Mikayla about the bizarre dream I had and get her input on it, but she's not there. I look up at the clock and it reads 9:25 am. All of these nightmares I've been having lately disturb my sleep, so I've been sleeping in a little bit later than usual. I've also been pretty tired lately in general, but I think that's a side-effect of the anti-depressant medication I've been taking since I got here.

I put my pen and paper back under my pillow and lay back down. It's kind of cool that I can write like that in my dreams. I was born to be a writer, it's the best thing about me, but the fact that I can write something so complex and detailed even when I'm unconscious takes serious skill. As I'm lying-in bed and staring at the popcorn ceiling, my eyes begin to open and shut sporadically. Just as my eyes begin to close and I feel myself sink back into slumber, I hear Mikayla come back into the room with Liv and Jessica.

"Guys, she's still sleeping, let's let her be," Liv says. She's so sweet, she's always so considerate of everyone.

"Let's jump on her and wake her up!" Mikayla says.

"No, that's mean," says Liv. Again, always so considerate.

"It's Tori, she won't be mad. Plus, we're just messing around," Jessica says. This can be kind of fun for me. I remain still with my eyes closed, but the floors in this unit are so damn creaky in certain spots, I can hear them walking towards me. Just as they get close to me, I jump up from my bed, stick my tongue out and scream as loud as I can! They all screamed back and jumped a mile like they've seen a ghost or something. I couldn't stop laughing.

"Got ya!" I yelled. They were still shaking. I was pretty impressed with myself, to be honest. I am definitely not a prankster, but that was fun.

"Damn Tori, you scared the shit out of us!" Jessica yelled, but I could tell she wasn't yelling out of anger.

"Well, you guys had it comin'!" I rebutted. She just stuck her tongue out and I smiled back at her.

All of the sudden, Mike and Andrew show up at our doorstep.

"Hey hey hey, what's all the ruckus ladies?" Mike exclaims, of course, with Andrew right behind him. Without me offering, Mike comes right in my room and takes a seat on my bed, right in front of my feet.

"Tori scared us," Liv replied.

"Um, she may have scared you guys, but I wasn't scared. I knew she was awake the whole time," Mikayla says.

"No way, you screamed the loudest out of all of us!" Jessica playfully snapped back at her. They both gave each other looks like "you know I'm right" when clearly Mikayla was wrong.

"I scared them all, no need to be embarrassed Mikayla," I teased as I winked at her.

"Nice work, Tori," Mike said as he put his hands up for a high five. Just as I was about to reciprocate the gesture, one of the nurses came over.

"Boys, you know you're not allowed to be in the girls room. Besides, it's time for morning medications anyway. Everyone to their rooms."

Suddenly, everyone dispersed and it was just me and Mikayla left in our room. Mikayla went to her bed while we waited for the nurse to come with our pills. One blue pill, one yellow pill, and one pink pill. Xanax, antidepressant, and birth control. Every day, at the same time, like clockwork. After the nurse watched me swallow pills, though, she said something she's never said before.

"Get changed, girls. After ten days, you've all earned outdoor privileges. It's a little crisp, I'd put a sweater on." The nurse walked out of our room to finish the medication rounds. I look over at Mikayla, who seemed just as shocked as I am.

"Really? We get to go outside?" I asked out loud.

"Well, it's about damn time, after keeping us locked up inside like lab rats. Let's go!" As soon as the words left her lips, we were up and changing so we could actually go outside! It almost seemed too good to be true. Something somewhat normal during all this chaos. And a reward for all of us working so hard is nice.

When we finished changing, we waited in our doorway for everyone else and the nurse who was going to bring us outside for what seemed like forever. Finally, it was time to go and pretty much everyone looked as excited as I was.

When we get downstairs to the hospital lobby, I can see the trees moving from the wind blowing. It might sound so ridiculous, but this was a big deal to me. It may have only been ten days, but it felt like a million. Time moves so slowly when you're not only battling yourself every day, but trying to better yourself too, especially when you're doing it while stuck in the confines of the same three different rooms twenty-four seven.

The nurse opened the doors and the six of us ran out there so fast you'd think we had been serving a life sentence in solitary confinement for three years. It felt like little kids being let out for recess. I breathed in the outdoor air, and let out the biggest sigh. Fresh air feels weird, but a good weird. I missed it. It's like that saying, you don't know what you got until it's gone. Mikayla was right, it was about damn time.

I just stood there in the sunshine and fall breeze. Everyone else ran over to the picnic tables to sit and talk, but I just stood still, soaking it all in. Nature has always been an important aspect of my life. The weather affects my body and my brain, and the environment around me always impacts my mental health. I lay down on the dry grass and look up at the clouds. I'm not the kind of person to see shapes in clouds, but sometimes I try to make sense out of a few.

"That one reminds me of you," I hear. I turn to my left and there's Mike lying next to me. I look back over at the group and see Andrew with the girls, not in Mike's shadow like he usually is. Good for him, maybe he's gaining some confidence in this place. I didn't even notice Mike came over here, though, I was so caught up in the sky and the clouds.

"How so?" I ask him.

"See that cloud there to the right? It's arced up on both sides and seems to cave in. It looks like a smile. And then do you see the wispy, smaller clouds on both sides? They look like dimples, which makes it your smile," He said while pointing to all the clouds he was referring to. I look over at him and am totally caught off guard, not sure what to reply. Naturally, I blush a little, and I think that was all the reply he needed.

"How have you been feeling?" I ask him. Typical guys like Mike aren't usually asked about their feelings. The tall, dark and handsome boys with muscles and an arm band tattoo don't like to show off emotions. It's not seen as 'manly' I guess to some people, but it's something I truly appreciate in anyone, no matter the gender. It's important that boys know they can share emotions too.

"I've actually been feeling okay. Levelled. Balanced. Medication really can work wonders sometimes. Who knew, right? That it really can get better if you just work for it," He replied.

"I'm happy for you, Mike. You deserve to feel better," I say with a smile. We look at each other for a few seconds, and then both look back up at the clouds.

"Thanks. How about you? How have you been feeling?" he asks me, and as his question comes to an end, I begin to feel his presence get closer to me. I can feel the sunshine coming off of his body and radiating onto me, and it feels different from the sunshine directly hitting me. It feels warmer, and it radiates through my body and my mind.

"I'm the same, just thinking differently at times. I still have the same sadness and sorrow within me. I always will, you know. Medication isn't going to change that. But what I think it's doing is helping me have a different thought process about certain things and helping me see certain situations from a different perspective. Dr S says that things aren't so black and white. That there is a lot of grey. I think the medication is helping me realise and acknowledge the grey, and know that there is a lot between life and death," I reply as I keep my gaze on the clouds. I can feel him looking at me again, but I just can't take my eyes off of the sky. Off of the clouds and the tall trees in my peripheral vision. I almost feel like I can't move.

"Things aren't going to be okay all the time, Tori. There will be good, and there will be bad, but you're right, there will be a lot of stuff in between too. I'm happy for you too," he says, and as soon as the words leave his lips, I feel his hand creep over and grab onto mine. Geez, I hope my hands aren't

163

too sweaty. Hello there again, my dear old friend anxiety has returned. For the first time in a while, though, it's a different kind of anxiety. I never thought I'd have butterflies in my stomach again, but feeling his touch in such a close, intimate way, I knew that's what was happening. That was the kind of anxiety. A weird, nervous, yet exciting, kind.

"It's a journey, all right. Do you ever wonder why were born this way though?

Why some people can just wake-up each and every morning and not have to try to be happy, they just naturally are? And then they go through their days thinking about their deadlines at work or what they are going to make for dinner. But then there are people like me. My thoughts each and every day can't be focused on things like that because they are too enveloped with just trying to stay afloat." As I finished speaking, I could feel the chills down my spine as he squeezed onto my hand tighter.

"You're just wired differently. We all are," he replied.

"Exactly. Don't you wonder why that is? Why it is so hard for us to do something as simple as be happy whereas other people don't have to fight for that feeling? I'm glad I'm getting help, but sometimes I still can't help but feel that it's almost like I'm being punished for something I did, maybe in another life. Or something I am going to do in this one. Do you ever feel that way?" I turn over a look at him as I finish talking, curious as to what he's going to say, if he's going to say anything, and he does, almost instantly.

"I used to sometimes, of course. Then my mom told me something that really resonated with me and made me think. She said that God only gives us what we can handle. He knows each of us so well that He knows exactly what each of our limits are. He knows exactly how many hairs are on each of our heads, and He knows exactly what we each of us are capable of," he said in the strongest yet calmest tone. What a powerful statement he just made. Naturally, I squeezed his hand even tighter and felt myself become closer to him, both physically and emotionally. He looked at me with a very strong expression. One that showed he really believed in what he was saying.

"You're religious?" I asked. I would have never guessed that. Again, this why you don't judge a book by its cover.

"Catholic Church on Sundays, Bible Study, Catholic school, the whole nine yards. What about you?"

"Catholic family and school. We only go to Church for special occasions and holidays, though. To be honest, I sort of lost my faith over the years with everything that's happened to me," I replied, somewhat shamefully.

"Well luckily, God always forgives those who ask for it and are open to it. I may not be the best, most God-like person there is, but I have to say, believing in Him and knowing that He's always there for me if and when I need Him, it's comforting," he said with a smile.

"That's good to know. Maybe I'll try to re-discover some faith when I get out of here," I said with a little smile back.

"Maybe I can take you to my Church sometime," he said to me, and I'm not totally sure why this time, but I felt myself begin to blush again.

"I'd like that," I say as I continue to blush more and more. I can feel him leaning in closer to me, and the butterflies in my stomach start going out of control. What is happening? Is he going to kiss me? What if he does and we get caught?

We're not supposed to get "close" to the people here. I understand why they don't want us to because of the kind of past these people remind us of but how can they expect us not to, though? We're going through the same things and understand each other. My mind is spinning out of control. Get it together Tori, he's about to kiss you! Focus, girl!

"Outdoor time is up, guys. Come line up!" the nurse screams out before she blows on her whistle. We got so startled that we both jumped up immediately and away from each other. No!!! You've got to be kidding me. Story of my life, right there. Once we both came back down from that adrenaline rush of shock, we both just looked at each other with one of those "Damn, better luck next time" kind of sad, side smiles. He was going to kiss me; it was so obvious. That damn whistle.

Mikayla, Jessica, Liv and Andrew walk towards us. Mike and Andrew break off in the front of the line and the girls and I make up the back. The three of them are chatting about something, but I couldn't focus enough to listen because I couldn't stop thinking about Mike and what happened and what just almost happened. Mikayla gave me a look like she could tell my mind was still in the clouds, but I just stood there and looked back at her with a blank stare, not showing the butterflies that were still fluttering around like crazy in my stomach, or the disappointment I was feeling that that moment had to end.

Chapter Fifteen
Night Eleven - Depression 101

As soon as we got back inside, I was the first girl to call for the shower. When I need to cry so loud that nobody could hear me, or I just need to think and be alone with my thoughts, the shower is the first place I go to. The hot water hitting my bare skin and no other sensation but that and my emotions, it just calms me. It's one of the only places I know I can totally just feel and not have to worry about anyone bothering me. That's how showers are at my home, I mean.

"Tori, five minutes left," the nurse calls to me from the other side of the door. Our showers here are limited to fifteen minutes. People who are on suicide watch have to shower with the nurse in the bathroom with you. It's always a nurse of the same gender and he or she would stand and face the corner while you showered.

The first few days I was here and on suicide watch, I refused to shower. I can't even write in peace; I wasn't letting them take my privacy to shower alone away too. No thank you.

Mike was going to kiss me. He was going to kiss ME. ME. Of all people. All of the girls here are nice and pretty and funny, what draws him to me? I never thought I would have any interest in anyone ever again after what happened to me the last time. Forget 'anyone' and 'ever again', if someone had told me that I was going to be interested in someone so quickly after what happened, and someone I met in a mental hospital, of all places, I would have told that person that he or she is absolutely insane. Who would have ever thought? Clearly, I'm a hopeless romantic, but meeting someone has been the last thing on my mind lately. I guess it's true what they say, that when you stop trying so hard, things naturally come to you.

I got out of the shower with barely a minute to spare. I wanted to use and take advantage of every second of my only alone time in this place. I needed to think and comprehend what happened outside and how I'm feeling about it. As I walk back to my room, I see Mikayla, Liv and Jessica through the glass pane of the hang-out room sitting on the couch talking. Mikayla was facing the hallway, and saw me heading back to our room. I saw her begin to get up as I entered our room. I turned around to put my towel down, turn back to face the corner, and there she was, almost instantly, like she sprinted over here or something, with that same look on her face that she had outside.

"So, what happened with you and Mike out there?" she asked me with a raised eyebrow, like she really wanted the scoop.

"You saw us?" I asked her. I figured she did, but I didn't want to disappoint her curiosity with the sad truth of the situation.

"Ummm, yeah. We all did. That's why we didn't come over there. So, you two lovebirds could have some alone time.

Well, semi-alone time in this place," she says. Ah, that explains why Andrew didn't come over with him.

"Lovebirds?" I asked. How did she know?

"Oh please, it's so obvious he is into you. And if I wasn't mistaken, I'd think you're into him too. And I'm never wrong," she said, so matter of fact that I couldn't even argue.

"I didn't know it was so obvious," I reply back.

"It's obvious on his end. And it's mostly obvious on your end when you blush. That's a dead giveaway."

"Yeah, that makes sense," I answered back shyly.

"You guys' vibe really well together. It's not a bad thing. Embrace it, girl. Did he make a move out there?" she asks with a quick wink and a smile.

"He held my hand. And then when I would speak, he would grab onto it tighter. And I'm 99.9% sure he went in to kiss me and as soon as I went in, the whistle blew and ruined everything!" Well, I didn't expect myself to say all of that, but I just couldn't stop. I need to remember to keep my tone in check and my voice down, this place is so damn small.

"My God, it's like a scene out of a movie! You guys are so totally going to get together!" Mikayla responds with excitement.

"I don't even know him outside of here, Mikayla."

"But you'll get to know him! This is just the jumping off point. And look at it this way: you both already know each other's biggest flaws, and you still like each other. That say's something, no?" she says as she looks at me like she's waiting for me to answer. She does make a good point. I haven't thought about that before.

Maybe that is a good thing. We may not know each other outside of here yet, but we know the most important things about who we are.

"Girls, it's time for group," The nurse calls to us from the hallway. Before I could give her an answer, the nurse interrupts us. These nurses really know how to pick timing today, like what the Hell. Mikayla and I walk towards the hang-out room and everyone else is already there. I sit down next to Liv and Mikayla sits down between me and Jessica. Mike and Andrew are sitting across from us.

"Hey," Mike says to me with a cute little side smile.

"Hi," I shyly reply back. Just then, Dr S walks in the room to start facilitating the group.

"Hello, beauties. Are we ready for group?" she asks.

"What are we doing today, Dr S?" Liv asks her.

"Today is going to be a simple creative writing group. You can write however you want, whatever you want. I'm going to pass out paper and pencils, and you can get started." Wow, I actually get to write in a public space? That's unheard of in this place. Thank God for "supervision" I guess.

"Dr S, I'm not a good writer," Andrew says.

"That's okay, Andrew. You aren't being judged or graded on this. Nobody will read it but you. Besides, as long as it comes from your heart, you are a good writer," she says back to him with a smile. Everyone gets their materials, and the room goes quiet.

Finally, I get to write without having to hide it. What an unusual feeling that has become. What to write about?

Sonnet? Nah. Too much structure. Freestyle? Nah. Not enough structure.

Haikus? That's a happy medium. Three lines, a five-seven-five syllable pattern. It doesn't require too much thinking, but has just enough challenge in it to keep it interesting. I like that.

I've always been told I'm a great writer and have a way with words. The reason for that is because it's relatable, and it's all things I connect with. It comes from my feelings and my emotions and the depths of my soul, but because of that, that also means it usually about something sad. Pain, sadness, what have you. It may be sad and somewhat concerning to some people, but it works for me. It's the healthiest outlet I have.

I close my eyes and my mind starts to go to work. Thinking of words, lines and phrases I could put together that fit the five-seven-five rule. After about five minutes or so, I think I got something. I pick up my pencil and begin writing:

Tears from Heaven

When the raindrops fall
They say that God is crying
That makes two of us.

I used to be a big crier. Sometimes I still can be, but not nearly as much anymore. Depression hits people differently, and sometimes, it even hits the same person differently. For example, I may not cry, but other people may cry all the time. Then there are days that I can't shed a tear, but then other days that I become one of those people who can't stop crying. It's complicated, really. You almost don't know who you are sometimes when you have depression. It can take over your personality. I don't think people on the outside looking in actually realise how hard it is to re-discover the person you were before depression took over. For someone like me who has had depression since childhood, sometimes you can't even remember if you had a personality or what you were once like because you didn't really have enough time to fully develop and embrace one. That's something I need to work on while I'm here: picturing a future for me without depression, because right now, that seems completely impossible.

"Fifteen minutes left, guys," Dr S says from the corner of the room. She looks like she's writing something of her own over there. She was always good about keeping herself involved and doing our therapy group activities with us. Fifteen minutes, I can probably get another haiku done. I start to think, and this time, my head goes to my ex. To be fair, that's where it usually goes lately when I'm trapped with my thoughts. That's another thing I really need to work on and figure out how to get under control. Five or so minutes later, I begin to write again:

Faltering Time

When you broke my heart
You said that time would heal it
So, I broke your watch

Fits perfectly, both in the poetic structure and my life. He used to always tell me that. "You'll get better" or "You'll be fine" or, my personal favourite, "As time goes by, you'll learn to be over me, you'll see." Is he crazy? Like I have some kind of on and off switch in my heart that can just decide what feelings to feel? He acts like it's so easy. He and I are in two completely different situations, but he refuses to see that. He has no idea. Just because he let me go so nonchalantly doesn't mean I can do it so easily.

Ugh, just thinking about him makes me so angry and sad all over again. I look up from my paper and see Mike. He's not even writing; he's just drawing a little cartoon stick figure or something. He must have been able to feel me looking at him, because he looked up at me and gave a me a little side smile and a wink. I could feel myself blushing again a little, like usual. He has such a good way of keeping my thoughts in check. Time may not have been working for me, but maybe another person could help?

"Times up, ladies and gents," Dr S says as she walks towards us.

"While it's not required, would anyone like to volunteer to read what they wrote out loud?" she asks. Not one peep.

"I would, but I didn't write anything Dr S." Mike said.

"Why didn't you write Mike?"

"I hit writer's block. But I did draw something that I don't mind sharing." "Okay, let's see it."

Mike holds his piece of paper up and starts to explain.

"So, these are two drawings of Tori. First, she's sitting there with her eyes closed, like she's really thinking hard about what she wants to write. Then the next one is of her looking down at her paper and actually writing it. It's her process."

"That's interesting, Mike. What made you want to draw that?" Dr S asks. "She's right in front of me, so she was the first thing that came to my mind.

And then her writing process inspired me."

You can hear a harmonious "oooooh" amongst the rest of the class, but I just sat there, embarrassed, but in a good way, so I'm sure I was blushing too.

"Oh class, enough. It's good that you guys are inspiring each other in here," Dr S says, winking at me. Little did she know what was really going on, but it's not like I could tell her. Friendships outside of here aren't really allowed, so forget any kind of other relationship.

"That's it for tonight, everyone. I hope that writing was a good release for you all and that whatever you wrote helped you in some way. Off to your rooms now, guys and gals. Goodnight!" Dr S says as she begins to leave the room. We all walk out and head to our rooms, but not before Mike sends another wink and cute smile my way. As he goes into his room, the girls come up to me straight away and cut me off in front of the doorway to my room.

"You're the first thing on his mind..." Mikayla says teasingly.

"You inspire him..." Jessica joins in. As usual, Liv just stood their smiling but I think didn't want to put me on the spot or make me feel embarrassed, so she didn't say anything.

"Oh please," I say back, also teasingly. Now Liv decides to chime in.

"You know you like him, Tori. You don't have to be embarrassed about it," she says, very sweetly.

"Thank you, Liv. I'm just confused. I'm still dealing with this massive heartbreak and the trauma it's left me with, I just don't know how I could even begin to try and commit to someone else when I'm not over that yet. I just need to think about it and figure out what I want and what I think I can handle," I say, and before any of the girls could respond, the nurse interrupts us.

"Girls, get to your rooms please."

Jessica and Liv head to their room and Mikayla and I go into ours. "Do you want to talk about it?" Mikayla asks.

"Not really. Thank you though." My mind was just so all over the place, and it was exhausting.

"Okay. Well, if you want to talk, you know where I sleep!" she said with a smile and a giggle.

"Thanks Mikayla, I really appreciate it," I said back with a smile.

How could I possibly even think about starting a new relationship when not only am I trying to work through this massive, still very fresh break-up, but there is also so much other stuff that I have to do to work on and better myself. I do like Mike though, it's just complicated. My brain hurts. I need to try and sleep, and hopefully, for once, get a good night's sleep. If only I did have a switch in my heart like my ex seems to think I do, I'd use it to not only turn my heart off, but my brain too. Then maybe I could actually get a decent night's sleep.

Chapter Sixteen
Day Twelve - The Poetry Book
I'll Never Write

There I am, standing on the side-lines, watching the world and the future I so desperately want happen in front of my eyes. There's a handsome man with his family; a beautiful woman and three kids. They are walking in the park on a beautiful, sunny day, all laughing and smiling together, as I sit there behind the shadows alone. All of the sudden, time flashes forward, and suddenly, I am a fly on the wall into the kid's bedroom. I see the couple tucking the kids into bed. With every bedtime story and kiss on the forehead, I shed tears, and then suddenly again, time flashes, and now, I'm left alone in a dark room. There I am, just standing there, looking into a mirror. I'm eyeing myself up and down when I start to panic. I slowly starting to give into the shortness of breath as I think about the events I witnessed and feel my heart break all over again. Stay Calm. Heart racing. Throat closing. Palms sweating. Body trembling. Breath shortening. Here it comes. Stay Calm.

Breathe In. Breathe Out. Breathe In. Breathe Out. Oh my God, just stay calm! Too late. It's happening. And I can't stop it. Fuck. Here we go again. I slam my fist hard against the

mirror, shattering the glass into a bunch of pieces. I watch as
the glass flies off the wall in slow motion and into my arm,
and the cuts they make spell out the words "Not Enough."

I spring up from my bed, breathing heavily and sweating profusely underneath my blanket. Who were these people? It didn't seem to be anyone I recognise, rather, a life I would like to live someday. That handsome man should have been him, and that beautiful woman should have been me, but instead it's complete strangers that I am left envious of. Why couldn't that be us? Will that ever be my life? Doubtful. Trying to calm myself, I look up to my old friends on the popcorn ceiling and begin counting.

One. Two. Three. Four.

Welcome back, dear friend anxiety, you even haunt me in my dreams. Five. Six. Seven. Eight.

Am I ever going to get a good night's sleep again? I look up at the clock and it reads 4:17 am.

"Ugh, this isn't working," I whisper to myself. I look over and see that Mikayla is still sleeping. I reach into the drawer of my nightstand and take out the emergency flashlight my mom gave me when I got here and pull out my pen and paper from underneath my pillow. Poetry always helps with my anxiety, especially the structured ones. They make me think and take my mind solely to that.

Double Tetractys

Trapped
Alone

Loneliness
All by myself
I'm doing pretty well, thanks for asking.
I've been able to catch up on TV
And my book too
Yeah, I'm fine
Being
Trapped

Breathe In, Breathe Out

You're my everything
Like the air, you surround me
You keep me breathing
But the air does not conform
Instead, it breathes itself in

What a Terrible Thing to Waste

My mind is so dark.
A place that should be full of dream.
Is the darkest place I've ever seen.
The imagination that once lived within me
Has been replaced with reality
And has become an impossible fairytale.
The light that used to spark my mind with hope
Has lately grown painfully dim
And now only suggests thoughts of sorrow.
It sits there, day in and day out
Controlling the way I live my life

They say a mind is a terrible thing to waste
But mine has become an agonising struggle
They say to let go of things that cause negativity
Yet my mind is something I cannot escape.
A mind is supposed to be a beautiful thing.
Where did mine go wrong?

All or Nothing

How do you expect me to love with a broken heart?
How do you expect me to breathe without air?
You were my heart
You were my oxygen
You were my everything
And now I'm nothing
How can you expect me to go on with nothing?
I can't
And I don't want to do it alone.

White Rose, Black Shadow

A great man once said
"He who does not trust enough
Will not be trusted"
But how do you know who to trust?
An innocent smile could be deceiving
A sweet gesture could be misleading
And a kind word could be teasing
It's difficult these days
To believe what people say

The past comes back to haunt you
And you recall the pain you've been through
And it's hard to trust someone again
You're afraid to again feel like a fool
But life does have some rules
And people need other people to live
So how do you let yourself trust again?
You put their trust to the test
Take it slow and hope for the best
Be cautious, but not nerved
Be careful, but not reserved
And go along for the ride
Don't forget though
Even a white rose casts a black shadow
And even the devil was once an angel

Why will I never write it? Because my poetry, as well as most of my writing, is mainly only about dark, deep and depressing stuff. Heartbreak, loneliness, sadness, etc. I mean, who would want to read about that? I don't even want to live it.

I look back up at the clock and now it reads 6:06 am. Damn, I better try to get some kind of actual sleep. I shove my pen and paper back under my pillow and put the flashlight away. I lay back down, close my eyes, and try to empty my mind. It never actually works, but I still try. What else can I do, right? I just want to sleep.

Brain, please let me sleep.

Chapter Seventeen
Night Twelve – The Dinner Crew

I'm sitting on the couch in the hang-out room, watching the girls play cards. Uno, to be exact, but it's a different type of Uno. It's called Uno Attack, and it comes with this machine that shoots out cards at you. When you have to draw cards, you hit the button and it randomly decides if and how many cards it's going to spit out at you. It can be anywhere from zero to like ten. It's fun, and kind of crazy.

That's one of the favourites here.

"Don't you want to play, Tori?" Liv asks.

"No thanks, Liv. I'm just going to watch," I reply, mid-yawn.

"You look like you haven't slept in centuries!" Jessica chimes in.

"I didn't sleep much last night," I reply, barely keeping my eyes open.

"I sleep amazing here!" Mikayla adds. Lucky her, I thought. I've haven't had a good night's sleep since day one of being here. They don't want to give me any kind of sleeping pills considering my "semi-addictive behaviour" as they put it, and in addition to all of the other medication I'm on, but still, I don't think that would even help. I've tried the stuff in the past to help me sleep, but sleeping can't even seem to turn off my brain. The nightmares come, and it's just like when I'm awake: constantly thinking. I'm sitting on the couch, thinking about how tired I am, and it's actually making me even more tired. Just as my eyes begin to shut, I'm startled.

"Attack!" Mikayla yells out as the Uno Attack machine shoots a huge handful of cards out at Jessica.

"Oh man, and I was so close to an Uno too!" Jessica says disappointedly. My eyes instantly spring open from the noise and standing in front of me, there's Mike, looking at me with one his signature half smiles. Embarrassed, I laugh a little back at him as his smile turns into slight laughter as well.

"Guys, it's time for dinner," Andrew says from the doorway

"Okay ladies, let's pause. Cards down, and no cheating!" Mikayla commands. Jessica rolls her eyes and they all begin to get up. Meanwhile, Mike is still standing over me as I don't want to get up from the couch.

"Come on, let's go," he says as he extends his hand out to help me up. I grab his hand and he pulls me up off the couch. As we begin to walk towards the door together, I realised that were still holding hands. I guess we both felt it at the same time because as we reached the door, we both let go at the same time.

"Whoops. Sorry," I said to him, feeling like I had to say something.

"Me too. I didn't even realise; it just feels so natural," he says back with a smirk and a wink. I look at him with a little giggle and lead the way.

"Come on, let's go." We walk into the dining room (again, it's really just a cafeteria, but the nurses here like to fancy it up by calling it a dining room) and everyone is already in their seats with their food. After the third meal together or so, everyone pretty much has assigned seats. It's one of those unwritten rule things; everyone just always sits in the same spot even though it was never really discussed.

I sit on one side of the main dining bench, with Mikayla on my right and Liv on my left. Across from me, Mike is right in front of me, with Andrew next to him on one side and Jessica next to him on the other.

Mike and I go and get our food and then go to our respective seats. "Spaghetti and meatballs again?" Mike says.

"I'm okay with that. I'm too Italian to ever get sick of carbs," I respond.

"Do you like the meatballs though?" Andrew asks.

"No meatball will ever beat my grandmother's, but for what they are, they're decent enough," I answer him.

"I like them, I think they're good!" Jessica says as she takes a bite and winks at me. Jessica has been getting better and better every day with her eating. Every meal, it seems like she's eating a little bit more and she's okay with it. I'm happy for her; she deserves that.

"So, Tori, why didn't you sleep last night?" Liv asks me.

"I don't know. I've been having a lot of nightmares lately, and they wake me up," I respond, with no other details.

"I've always slept a lot, I love it. I can't imagine being up all night. Not sure I could function properly on less than eight hours," Mike says.

"Yeah, the nights can be long sometimes," I reply.

"Not too long though when you're writing," Mikayla says with a wink. "What do you mean?" I ask her, wondering how she knew about that.

"I woke up in the middle of the night last night and saw you with your pen and paper and flashlight," she says, a little too loudly for my taste.

"Mikayla, shhh! Please. Nobody say anything," I plead to everyone.

"Of course not. It's not like you're hurting anyone or yourself. God the rules here make no sense, it's ridiculous! We should be able to have the right to express ourselves creatively. I may suck at it, but still!" Andrew argues. Wow, I've never heard him get so heated about something. Sometimes I forget that he has a bipolar disorder. That may have been the closest thing I've ever seen to him getting mad. The meds he's on here must really help to mellow him out and keep him calm. He's right, though, I could be doing and sneaking something much, much worse than writing, trust me.

"Yeah, sometimes the rules here are over the top. I guess it's for our safety though, in some way. They have to think of everything here since they are responsible for us," Liv replies. She's also right, but that doesn't make it any less annoying.

"Tori, I didn't know you liked to write so much," Jessica says.

"You were probably really happy about yesterday's group," Liv added. "What do you write about?" Mike asks. Who knew everyone would be so interested?

"Umm, anything, really. Whatever I'm thinking about. Whatever I'm feeling.

It's a good, healthy outlet for me. I enjoy it," I answer.

"So, it helps you when you feel like you want to do something bad?" Liv asks. I know she's referring to cutting, but I think she was afraid for the rest of the gang to know that she struggles with self-harm.

"Yeah, it definitely has," I look at her and respond, trying to give her some comfort and reassurance.

"Maybe you'll write a book someday!" Jessica exclaims.

"Yeah! How cool would that be? And we'd all be friends with an author? SO cool!" Andrew says, and the rest of the group agrees. I've never seen him so excited before. It was then that I realised that these people are my friends, and that they consider me a friend. I haven't had friends in so long, I almost forgot what it felt like. To be totally myself and honest with people and trust them not to judge me for it. Just then, Dr S walks in and comes over to us.

"Hi everyone! Are we all having a good day?"

"Yes ma'am! We were just talking about yesterday's writing group," Mikayla responds.

"I'm glad. Did you guys enjoy it?" she asks us all collectively.

"It was something different. I don't write a lot, but it may be something to try more and get into," Liv answers.

"You can ask Tori about it. She's a big writer, you know," Dr S says to Liv as she smiles over my way.

"Yeah, she was just telling us," Jessica says.

"I don't know. Tori said she writes about what she's feeling and thinking. For me, that would be a lot of negative stuff," Andrew says.

"It would probably be like that for many people, Andrew, but sometimes, getting it out on paper can help release it from your mind," Dr S says.

"I guess that makes sense," Andrew responds back.

"Well, enjoy the rest of your dinner guys. I'll see you all tomorrow," Dr S says. We all say our goodbyes, and she walks out of the room.

"I like Dr S. a lot," Andrew says, and the rest of us nod in agreement.

"I do too. I am going to miss her when I leave here," I respond. I can't believe this is my second to last night here already. The beginning went by so slow, but now that it is almost time to leave, I almost can't believe it. It's a little stressful to think about right now. Welcome back, my good friend anxiety. I'm working on keep our relationship a little more distant these days, but you always like to weasel your way back to me somehow.

Everyone finishes up their dinner and cleans up their plates. There was nothing planned for us tonight, so we all got to hang-out together again in the hang-out room. Down time is nice, but also important, especially when I'm this tired and don't want to think too hard about anything right now.

"Okay, ladies, back to our game," Jessica says.

"Yeah, back to me kicking your butt!" Mikayla exclaims, as Jessica rolls her eyes at her, yet again. That's become a pretty common way for Jessica to respond to Mikayla now. All teasingly, with love, of course. The three girls sit down to finish their game and I go back to my spot on the couch. This time, Mike and Andrew sit down next to me. We sit there and watch the girls play, all the while, I can feel Mike's hand inching closer and closer to mine, just like when we were outside. We were sitting close enough that nobody could see it, but he eventually reached for my hand, and I held it back.

I tried to not think about it, but the thought of me leaving in just one more day creeps its way back to me. All of the sudden, I feel like I am in an out of body experience. I came into this, severely depressed and suicidal, and while that's always going to be a part of who I am, I'm leaving here with so much more. I feel like I'm floating. I see Mikayla, Liv and Jessica playing their game and me, Mike and Andrew sitting on the couch. In the beginning, I never thought I'd be open to getting close to these people, especially Mike. I'm going to miss them more than I ever thought I would. I suddenly snap back into myself when I hear Liv's voice.

"Uno!" she exclaims, and a few moves later, she plays her last card and wins the game. Good for her, she rarely ever wins.

"Tori, come on, come play with us!" Mikayla pleads.

"Yeah, come on, we'll deal you in," Jessica adds.

There's only so much time I have left here, I should be enjoying it with my new found friends. Don't get me wrong, I know I have to get back to real life sooner or later, but I am going to miss this (I never thought I'd say that).

"Alright, you're on! Mike, Andrew, come on, let's all play," I say as I pull Mike towards the girls. Andrew follows, the two agree, and its game on. Jessica shuffles and deals the cards and we start to play. I skip Mike, Mike makes Mikayla hit the button, and she gets three cards. The game goes on, and suddenly, my mind takes a step back and realises that for the first time, in a really long time, I'm actually having fun, and there is a genuine smile on my face and a real laugh coming out of me. I'm happy that I'm working on myself and getting myself better, but I wonder if I would be as far as I am in that process without these five other people sitting around me. Or

Dr S. Or even the nurses here. I've always tried to be strong for everyone around me and do everything on my own, but I've come to learn that it's really true what they say: people need other people, and that's completely okay.

Chapter Eighteen
Day Thirteen –
Goodbye, Sweetheart

"Tori, you there?" Dr S. says as she looks at me with a puzzled look on her face. Oh geez, who knows how long she was sitting in front of my face trying to get my attention.

"Yeah, sorry. My heads been in the clouds all morning. I'm here now," I reply. I wasn't just making up an excuse, I've really been out of it this morning.

"Where in the clouds?" she asks. I just sit there, thinking about what to say, but I guess I took too long, because she asks another question.

"How are you feeling about going home tomorrow?" What a loaded question, with an answer I never thought I'd say.

"Good, but also a little nervous,"

"It's okay to be nervous. That's a very common feeling for a lot of teenagers when they leave. They are excited to have some normalcy back in their life but they are also nervous about how they are going to handle it. Will life be better now that I've been through the program at St Vincent's? Will I be able to handle hardships better? What if I'm not as okay as I think I am and I go back into the real world and mess up and end up back here anyway?" Oh, my goodness, how does Dr S. always do that? This woman reads my mind like she's supernatural. I've really grown to like Dr S. She's really helped me, and honestly, I didn't think that was possible. I never thought I'd be able to talk to someone openly and honestly the way I do with her. If she didn't judge me for what I put in those notes, there's not much else for her to judge me for.

"That's pretty much exactly everything I've been feeling, yes. I already have an extremely hard time feeling like I am enough, I don't want to fail again," I respond to her.

"The concerns are normal Tori. The truth is, real life is going to be the same. You are going to have to deal with the same life events that got you here in the first place, and more things are going to happen that are going to test you.

The reality is that real life didn't change, you did. You are going to leave here tomorrow more equipped than ever before to handle life and tackle whatever it has to throw at you as a healthier and stronger you. You have to have faith and trust in yourself that you're growing, and you are a very different person leaving here than you were coming here," she says back to me.

"That kind of freaks me out, though," I reply.

"What does?" she asks.

"The whole 'different person thing'."

"And why do you think that is?"

"My life started to change when I was in the seventh grade. That's when the intense bullying started, and since then, so many other horrible and negative things have happened to me. I have been struggling with my depression and anxiety and this deep self-hatred for so long now. And other things have developed, like the cutting and suicidal ideation, and it's only gotten worse. I was too young to really remember my life or myself before bad things started happening and before I became clinically depressed. I don't know who I am if I'm not like this. I don't know how to re-discover the person I was before all of this, and honestly, I'm scared to try. I don't know my personality without my mental health issues. I've had all this come on at such an early age in my life that I don't even know if I have my own personality. I don't even feel like I had any time to be a person before my depression and anxiety and everything else started. It's scary, having no idea who I truly am," I just look at her as I finish talking and I can tell by the way her eyes are locked on me that she is really listening and hearing what I'm saying.

"Tori, you are one of the most self-aware teenagers I have ever met. You have come so far and have learned a lot about yourself. When your anxiety is being triggered, when you're starting to feel sad, etc. Change is a very scary thing for most people, and this is a big change. I know that you do not know the person beneath all of the negative thing's life has thrown your way, but even though you don't, I do. I know that there is a person under there behind the shadows of depression waiting to be set free. I know that she is a strong, beautiful, and capable person, with a wonderful personality, and that she will flourish as her new self with her new skills to tackle the world," she responded. I could tell by her tone that she truly believed it.

"How can you know that?" I ask.

"Because I've seen that person. I've seen glimpses of her here. The way you genuinely care for all of the other teenagers here. The way you try to push them to better themselves, because you believe that they are capable of feeling better, and that they deserve to. And the way that they gravitate towards you shows a lot about you as a person too. And that's a pretty wonderful person to me," she answered with a smile.

"It is nice to be liked here. I've never really been that regular girl with friends. Here I'm not the fat girl, or the bullied girl, or the ugly girl. I can be myself here with these people, and that's something I truly appreciate about them, that I am not seen as those things that the rest of the world sees me as. I'm going to miss being that girl when I leave here," I reply, trying to hold back the tear I feel trying to creep out of my right eye.

"The way people feel about and treat you says more about them than it does about you. I know how hard it is to not take things like that personally, as it's only natural, but it reflects how they truly feel about themselves. There are going to be people that hurt you all your life, but there will also going to be people like the friends you made here that will appreciate you for you, and you will be enough for them." That was a big statement. My whole life I've never been enough for anyone. I don't know if I'll ever truly be enough for someone, but she has a point.

"I've just naturally always wanted to help people. I think that I have been through so much and have been at such a lonely, rock bottom place in life that I don't want anyone to have to go through what I did," I respond.

"That right there says a lot about you, Tori. That's the person underneath all of your mental health issues. She's there, that's you. She's fighting to come out. And we are going to let her to come out and shine," she says back with a smile, and then continues on.

"You believe all of these other kids here that they are worthy and deserving of happiness and recovery. Now it's time you believe that about yourself, because you are just as deserving of those things as they are. I see it, they see it, it's your turn to see it," she says with a wink at the end. I guess she picked up on the fact that I didn't really know how to respond, so she spoke again.

"And you won't be alone, Tori. I'll be there to help you the whole time." "Really? We're still going to talk when I leave?"

"Of course. If you want to," she answers with a smile.

"Yeah, I think I'd like that," I respond with a halfway smile of my own. "Terrific. Well then, you're stuck with me, kiddo!" she says with another wink, and then continues on.

"So, what else is going on, sweetheart? Anything else you're concerned about leaving here with?" I didn't want to tell her about Mike just yet. We are not really 'allowed' to share numbers and keep in contact with people outside of here once we leave. I somewhat understand that, because it may bring you back to a tough time, or the person's mental health issues can trigger yours, maybe. At the same time though, with what we are all going through and that type of bond that we share, I don't know how they expect us to not get close and make friendships. I don't know. Regardless, it just didn't feel like the time. I'm not even sure what I'd even say anyway at this point in regards to the situation. Who knows what will happen and where we will stand after I leave tomorrow.

"I've been having nightmares pretty frequently," I tell her.

"Really? Tell me about them."

"Sometimes they are about things I've been through in my past, like traumatic events and stuff. Other times, they are random, and I'm not sure what specifically triggers them," I tell her.

"Tell me about the last one."

"It was about him. I saw him with a family, living a life with a woman that wasn't me. It was torture. Like having my biggest fear and nightmare thrown in my face. I know that's never going to be me, and at this point, I don't even know what I would do if he did end up choosing me. That's not going to happen, though, so I try not to think about the what if's anymore," I tell her, while looking at the ground again.

"Have you always been prone to nightmares?" she asks.

"I have, but they seem to be more often since I've been here," I answer. "You're going through a lot in here and handling emotions that you've shoved deep down inside and tried to suppress due to the extreme amount of pain they cause. While you've been here, you've been bringing those feelings to light, trying to work through them. That is not an easy thing to do, and now that they are being said out loud and being acknowledged and becoming more real, it makes sense that your mind becomes fixated on them now, even while you're sleeping." Everything she's saying makes total sense.

"When I was at my lowest, my life felt like I was living in a nightmare, and sleep was the only way to escape from it. My mind thinks and thinks and never shuts up except for when I'm sleeping, but now, the nightmares are increasing, and I can't even stop thinking then. I just want a break sometimes from thinking about everything, ya know?" I ask.

"Absolutely. Everyone needs and deserves a break. Like I said, I think a lot is being brought up during your stay here, and that as you work through some of these traumatic experiences, the nightmares will lessen. As time goes on and you conquer the trauma and deal with the feelings it causes you, your brain won't feel the need to think about it as much, and you won't have as many frequent nightmares about it." Again, everything she's saying makes total sense.

"That makes sense," I assure her. "I guess it's like that saying 'it's going to get worse before it gets better'," I add.

"That's exactly it. And it will get better, I promise you. In the meantime, I am going to add Melatonin to your nightly meds, and we will get through this together," she says back with a smile, and I feel myself naturally nod and smile back at her.

"Is there anything else you want to talk about today?" she asks. I shrug my shoulders, still not wanting to talk about Mike yet. Baby steps, ya know. I'm still getting adjusted to this whole "talking" thing. She starts to get up, so I follow suit, and before I know it, she's standing there in front of me with her arms out, waiting for a hug. I meet her embrace, and as usual, she's practically towering over me in her six-inch heels. This time they were red pumps, but just as tall. I'm not totally sure why, but a tear ran down my cheek as I hugged her. As I pulled away, I wiped the tear away, hopefully before she noticed it, but nothing usually gets by her.

"Thank you for everything," I say. She truly has helped me get to this next phase of my life and my recovery, and without her, I don't think I'd be ready and willing to be hopeful again.

"Hey, you did all the work. I just guided you along the right path. You should be very proud of yourself, Tori. I know

I am," she says back with a warm smile, and I nod back with one my signature half embarrassed, half genuine smiles.

"Go enjoy your last night, sweetheart. You deserve it," she adds. I turn back around towards the door and for the last time, I see, in bold, black letters, the word "SAFEZONE" with a red checkmark next to it. In the beginning, this place couldn't feel more unsafe for me, but as time went on, Dr S and this boring, plain, 'exactly as you'd expect' therapist's office, truly did become a safe zone for me, and I'm really grateful for that.

I open the door, but turn back around to face Dr S. again. "Wait! I do have one more thing I want to talk about," I exclaim. "Shoot."

"What does the S stand for?" I ask. She looks at me and giggles. It was a random question, and I've completely lost count of how many times she used the word sweetheart since I got here, but still, I'm curious.

"Interesting question. Tell ya what, once you get out of here tomorrow, at the end of our next session, I'll tell you," she answered with a wink. Always leave them wanting more, I guess? I honestly couldn't tell you what that was all about, but I guess for now, she'll just have to stay Dr Sweetheart to me.

Chapter Nineteen
Night Thirteen – One Close, Loving Family

By the time my therapy session was over, I knew that everyone would already be in the dining room. I head over there and see everyone but Andrew sitting at the table. It's in this moment as I look at them all that I fully realise that it's the last time, for a while, at least, that we are all going to be having a meal together. Hopefully we can figure out how to all see each other outside of this place, even though it's kind of frowned upon, but that also depends on when they all leave and how well they navigate their own lives outside of here. I have faith in all of them, though, I know they can do it. Who would've thought I'd really grow to care about these people so much? Not me, that's for sure. We went from one small, mentally ill family to one close, loving family, and that's definitely not something that I ever expected to happen in here.

I walk into the dining room and wave as I pass the table to get in line and get my food. Spaghetti and meatballs? Being 100% Italian, it's so hard to eat Italian food that's not prepared by my mom, Granny or Nonna, but especially in a hospital cafeteria. I am definitely going to miss these people, but one thing I will not miss: the food.

I take my food over to the table and join everyone. Before my butt barely hits the chair, I don't even have time to greet everyone before we're all startled.

"Guys! I think I'm going home on Friday!" Andrew says with excitement as he runs into the room and sits down right next to me. I haven't heard him talk so loudly and gleefully before; it was nice to hear that tone from him.

"Really? That's so exciting!" I respond to him.

"Congrats Andrew!" Liv says next.

"Dr S and I spoke this morning and she seems to think I'm ready. Then she called my mother and spoke to her, and now it's official," he replies with a smile.

"I'm happy for you, but I'm going to miss you!" Mike chimes in.

"I'm happy for all of you, but it's sad that all my friends are leaving," Mikayla adds with a sad look on her face.

"Hey, you'll still have me!" Jess says rebuts.

"Gee, great," Mikayla responds to her in a sarcastic tone and an eye roll. "Hey!" Jess barks.

"I'm just kidding, Jess. Duh!" Mikayla says back with a wink. Then she continues to speak.

"Still, though, you know what I mean. We've all gotten so close, and now we have to be split up again. And we have to deal with the real world outside of here without each other."

I didn't realise that Mikayla was so worried. I guess Dr S was right, and the emotions that I'm feeling are pretty common.

"We are still going to be there for each other, no?" Liv asks.

"Hey, of course we are," I answer right away.

"I don't care what it takes, we are not going to lose each other. We've each lost enough in this life, don't you think?" I rhetorically ask the table.

"I'm not losing you," Mike whispers under his breath, thinking nobody heard him. I don't think anyone else heard him, but I did. I look at him and he winks at me, and I have to tell myself not to blush.

"It's going to be okay guys. We got this," Andrew adds before getting up from the table to get his dinner.

"So, Tori, what's the first thing you are going to do when you get home tomorrow?" Jess asks.

"Hug my dog, hands down. Not even a question," I respond. Being around animals always makes me feel better. The way they have such unconditional love for us and no judgement, it's just an incredible feeling.

"And ask my mom to make me some real spaghetti and meatballs. Definitely," I add as I twirl the hospital spaghetti on my plastic fork with an undesired look. Everyone giggles a little, and it's even funnier because it's true.

Andrew comes back to the table and starts eating his dinner. I look over at Jessica, and her plate is almost empty. I'm so proud of her. I look down at my plate, however, and it's barely been touched. I'm not hungry, nor does my food look appetising.

"Aren't you going to eat more, Tori?" Liv asks, like she could read my mind.

"I'm not hungry," I respond. Too much going on in my mind right now.

"Can I have it? I'm happy, and I feel like eating, even if it's this," Andrew asks me. I can definitely relate to that feeling. I nod and push my plate over to him. As I do so, Mike picks up his empty dinner plate, walks over to the garbage can and throws it away. Then he walks over to me and puts his arm out, like he's waiting for me to grab it.

"Care to join me in the hang out room, Tori?" he asks me, still with his arm out. I let out a little smile and reach up with my good arm to grab his.

"I'd be delighted," I say back, playing along. I didn't want Dr S or any hospital worker seeing us arm in arm, so I let go once I got up, and I could tell by his look at that he understood and knew why. As we walk out of the dining room together, I hear the girls behind me with a quiet, ominous "oooooooh". Again, I don't think anyone else heard it, but I did. I look back at them and give them a look that says "oh please" with just my eyes as they giggle back at me.

Mike and I get to the hang out room and sit on the couch together. My palms feel a little sweaty, and instantly, those butterflies in my stomach are back, and going crazy, I might add. Again, I never thought I'd care so much about these people, especially him, given how my first impression of him went. I'm glad I was able to forgive him and give him another chance.

"I have something I want to give you, Tori," he says to me as he reaches into his pocket. How could he have gotten me anything in here?

"Really? That's so sweet," I respond. The butterflies are really going nuts inside my stomach. My old friend social anxiety makes its way back. Welcome back, dear friend.

He reaches into his pocket and pulls out a crumpled-up, balled-up tissue. That's odd. He hands it to me, and once I'm holding it, I can feel that something is wrapped in it. That's not so odd anymore. It's kind of cute, actually.

I open up the tissue, and inside of it is a keychain. It's a circular emblem, and on it is a picture of a beach with footprints in the sand. I flip it over, and on the other side, it is engraved with the words: "When you saw only one set of footprints, it was then that I carried you." Before I can say anything, Mike put his hands over mine and begins to speak.

"This is a quote from a prayer. It's the Lord telling you that when you are going through hard times and feel that He is not there for you, He is always there, even though you can't see it. Sometimes He walks beside you, and other times, He needs to carry you through the difficult times to get you to the better times that lie ahead. Either way, He's always there," he says to me with the sweetest smile I have ever seen. I look up at him and a tear runs down my cheek. I don't know why I'm crying, honestly. There's so many feelings and emotions going on in my head and in my heart, and I'm just overwhelmed.

"Mike, this is the nicest gift anyone has ever given to me. Thank you."

"You're welcome, Tori. That prayer has helped me get through some tough times in my life. I've carried it around with me for years now, and when I found out I was being sent here, I felt I had to sneak it in here and have it with me, and now I know why," he says, still with that same, sweet smile on his adorable face.

"Are you sure you want me to take this from you?" I ask him.

"I couldn't be more sure. I want you to have it," he answers as he nods.

"I'll cherish it forever," I respond as I lean in to hug him. I wrap my good arm around him and squeeze tightly onto him. It may have been too tight, but I didn't care. I couldn't help it. He hugs me back, and in that moment, I swear, the world stood still. I wasn't thinking about leaving tomorrow. I wasn't thinking about my depression or my ex or my dear friend social anxiety coming back to visit me. I wasn't thinking about the fear I was having about going back into the real world. All I could think about was this moment, and it felt amazing.

As I finally pull away from the hug, our faces are inches apart. I almost got lost in that moment, like a trance, but I snapped back into reality. I began to separate myself a little more, but just as I went to do so, Mike put his hand on my cheek. As he caressed it, the butterflies in my stomach are going absolutely wild, and I had the same feeling that I had when we were laying down outside together a few days ago. Before I could think much more about what I was feeling and what was happening, Mike moves in even closer to me, and plants his lips directly on mine.

As soon as his lips touched mine, even slightly, it was like a lightning bolt went through my entire body. Like fireworks went off in my stomach, making the butterflies go that much crazier. I've never felt chemistry or a connection like this with anyone, and it's that exciting kind of nervous again. It was like a first kiss story that you see in the movies, and it was absolutely perfect.

Mike pulls out of the kiss and looks at me with his sweet smile. Geez, that smile melts me.

"Sorry. Was that, okay?" he asks. Okay? It was freaking amazing!

"Don't be sorry," I answer with the most blushed face he's probably ever seen. I smile back, lean in and squeeze onto the keychain in my hand as I give him a kiss on the cheek.

"Thank you again for the gift," I say, still smiling, probably looking like a lovestruck idiot, but I couldn't help it. We look into each other's eyes, and I could feel a second kiss coming on, if not from him, then definitely from me. Again, I couldn't help it. Welcome back, social anxiety. Join the party! I don't care, this lovestruck feeling is definitely overpowering you right now. Sorry, not sorry.

Just as we both lean in, we hear the rest of the group coming, and instantly pull away from each other. I think the girls could sense what was going on, because Mikayla spoke up.

"Are we interrupting something?" she asks with that suspicious tone of voice that says she already knew the answer to her question.

"No, it's okay. I'll be right back," I answer as I get up off the couch, leave the hang out room and go towards my bedroom. I haven't felt this feeling in a long time, I almost forgot what it feels like. Loving someone and feeling loved, it's indescribable. I go to my room and sit on my bed, still smiling, still probably looking like an idiot. I pull out my pen and paper, and the words just naturally flow.

Just Us and the Moon

Do you ever look up at the Moon?
And wonder who's staring at it with you?
A different place, and a different face

203

But the same moment
Knowing that someone somewhere is staring at it too?
You don't know who
And you don't know why
But you can feel their eyes gazing
And that oddly unfamiliar
Yet wonderfully similar connection
Just simply feels amazing
You can feel them gaze into the Moon, as are you
And whether they are near or far
You are in this moment together
And you realise that you aren't as alone as you may feel
And suddenly, that connection becomes real
Out of seven billion people, you may only be one
And in comparison, to the Moon, you may be small
But when you think about someone, somewhere
Gazing into the light of the Moon with you
You realise you aren't just a small 'one' after all
You don't know this person
And they don't know you
Yet you perfectly harmonise in sync
Like Beethoven's Symphony No. 2
Within the same rhythm
And within the same tune
Possibly from the other side of the world
Unknowingly sharing this one moment together
Simply by looking up at the Moon.

"Tori, are you okay?" I hear in Mike's voice coming from outside the door "Yep, I'm good. I'll be there in a minute," I answer, and I hear him walk back down the hallway. How sweet of him to come check on me.

I never thought I'd feel this way again. Like I met the person who stares at the moon the same time as I do. And it's incredible. After what happened to me already, I didn't think that person actually existed. And I never thought that I would've met that person right after hitting the lowest point in my life. Little did I know that he was waiting for me here at St Vincent's Hospital.

Chapter Twenty
Day Fourteen –
What Does C Stand For?

Two weeks. Day Fourteen. It's actually here.

I look up at the clock and it reads 10:25 am. I spent the morning packing up my stuff in the hospital bags they give us. The bags aren't that big, but it's the only way we are allowed to take our stuff out of here. We also weren't allowed to bring anything in without it all being in those bags. That nicely organised suitcase my mom packed up for me got messed up and rummaged through really quick.

Everything we brought in had to be checked twice, first by security and then again by the ward nurses, so I guess it's easier for them if we have everything in extra sturdy plastic bags.

As I finish packing, I still can't believe I am actually going home today. I sit down on my bed and look around the room with these mixed feelings that I never would have expected to have. Will I miss this place? No, not really. But will I miss these people? Definitely. The people here really have helped and changed me, and I'll never be able to thank them enough for that. Dr S. always reminds me to give myself credit too, which I've been working on, but without her and the friendships I've made here, I wouldn't be in a position where I'm even able to give myself credit. Still sitting on my bed, I look up at the popcorn ceiling and count for the final time.

One. Two. Three. Four.
I can't believe it's been two weeks.
Five. Six. Seven. Eight.
I can't believe I survived.
Nine. Ten. Eleven. Twelve.
I can't believe I thrived.

My counting is interrupted by a knock on the door. I snap out of my counting and look over to see Mikayla in the doorway.

"Hey roomie. I can still call you that for the next hour or so," she says.

"You can always call me that, Mikayla," I respond back with a half-smile. "Okay, good. I was honestly probably going to anyway," she replies as she shrugs her shoulders while she comes over and joins me in sitting on my bed. "I'm going to miss you, Queen Victoria," she says.

"I thought that was historically inaccurate. Is your mind slipping?" I ask in an obviously joking tone.

"Nah, but you are pretty queen-like, so I'll pretend like I don't know that historically interesting tidbit and give it to you," she answers me as she looks over at me with a smile. I smile back, not really sure how to say thank you. I've never been good at taking compliments. I guess that's something I have to work on too. Just add it to the list. Might be lengthy, but why stop trying now?

"Do you know if you're getting a roommate?" I ask her.

"I don't know. I hope not, but even if I do, it won't be for long," she answers.

"What do you mean?" I ask.

"I just finished my session with Dr S. She's sending me home next week," she answers in a weirdly calm tone.

"Dude that's awesome! Aren't you happy?" I exclaim.

"Yeah. It just doesn't feel real. And I hope I'm as ready to leave here as she thinks I am," she responds back in the same tone.

"I get that. It still doesn't even feel totally real to me yet," I respond.

"Do you feel ready?" she asks.

"Last night I did. This morning I don't. But Dr S says that's normal. We're going to question ourselves, but she always tells me to acknowledge the work I've put in to get here and have faith in myself. It's not easy, but it's solid advice."

"Dr S. always gives good advice."

"Yeah, she does."

There's a small gap in our conversation, but it wasn't an awkward silence.

Trust me, I know what those feel like way too much. This was different. I look over at her and can tell she's hard at work in her mind, thinking about a lot. I put my hand on her knee and smile at her as big as I can as she looks over at me.

"I'm proud of you, Mikayla. You should be too," I say.

"Thanks, roomie," she says as she gives me a hug. I am really going to miss her. Who knew after that first awkward encounter that we'd grow to become to such good friends? As we both release from our hug, I hear another voice coming from the doorway. This time, it's a male voice.

"Tori, you have a minute?"

I look over at the door and see Mike standing there. Before I can say anything, Mikayla raises her eyebrows at me, gets up off the bed and walks out the door, past Mike and into the hallway.

"Sure."

He walks in and takes Mikayla's place on my bed. He leans in and kisses my cheek so sweetly and I instantly begin to blush but do my best to control it (if that's even possible).

"So, you all ready to go?" he asks.

"I don't know," I answer hesitantly.

"You got this, Tori. You're such an inspiration, and you can do anything," he responds to me and if I was controlling the blushing before, I'm definitely not now.

"You think so?"

"I really do. Look at what you've been through, and you're still standing to tell the tale. You're fighting through all the pain, working harder than ever, and you're doing the damn thing," he responds with that signature sweet smile across his face that just melts my heart every single time.

"That means a lot. Thank you," I answer as I feel my hand grab onto his. "So, where do we really go from here? I mean, I don't want really know what's going on with us, but I don't want it to end," he says. Welcome back social anxiety, my dear friend. I'm learning how to befriend you a little bit more.

"I don't either. Obviously, I'm still dealing with the pain and heartache from my ex, but I don't want to lose what we have either. I just don't know how serious I can be until I fully deal with that, you know?"

I am such a people pleaser that saying "no" is not something I do often, but with Mike, I just feel like I can be totally myself and honest with him. He and I are similar in many ways, and I can tell by the person he is that, like me, he appreciates honesty in people.

"There's no pressure here. We don't have to rush into anything. I just don't want to lose our friendship," he responds with a smile and another kiss on the cheek.

"Whatever is meant to be, will be," he adds with a wink as he gets up off of my bed and stands in front of me. He looks over at the clock and then back at me.

"11:11. Make a wish," he says. I close my eyes and go for it.

I wish for strength. That when I leave here, I will be strong enough to navigate the world and handle whatever life has to throw at me in a healthier way.

I wish for courage. That I will be brave enough to challenge myself in the world, put my trust into other people and have faith in myself that I can do this.

I wish for self-love. That I will be able to show myself the comfort, support and gentleness that I deserve and begin to see myself in a brighter light as others do.

I wish for happiness. That one day, my life can be more about finding the light rather than being stuck in the darkness. That I can find genuine joy in my life and revel in the happiness, whatever that may mean or be.

I wish for all that, and so much more. If I've learned anything from being here, it's that it takes more than just a wish. I know it takes effort and drive to make your wishes come true, but still, wishing on a shooting star or a clock that reads 11:11 can't hurt. I'm pretty sure it's technically only one wish per 11:11 moment, but oh well, I'm going for it.

"Did you wish for something too?" I ask.

"I didn't need to. Mine already came true," he says with another wink and that sweet smile that I am going to miss. I don't know when I'm going to see it again.

Still standing in front of me, Mike puts his arms out for me to grab onto. He grabs onto me and as he lifts me up off of the bed, he kisses me again, but this time, on my lips. It's a quick peck, but still, in that short moment, I could feel that lightning bolt again, just like the first time. That kiss leads in a hug, and it may have been the best hug ever. His smell, his touch, and it was just all so comforting in a time where I really need some. I could tell that neither of us really wanted to let go, but we knew that eventually we'd have to.

"Here, this is for you," I look down and Mike has his hand out with a piece of paper in it. I open it up and inside are everyone's names written down, and next to each one is a phone number and email address. We're technically not allowed to exchange contact information, so I quickly put the piece of paper in my pocket and as I do so, I nod and smile back at Mike. He winks at me, and speaks up again.

"Come on, let's go. Everyone wants to see you," Mike says as he turns around and heads for the door. I follow his lead and we head out into the hallway.

Walking through the hallway for one of the final times with Mike, I still can't believe the day has come for me to leave, and I still can't believe how far I've come.

We get to the hang-out room and the rest of the group is sitting on the couch and on the floor around the coffee table, playing our favourite game, Uno Attack. As soon as we walk in, everyone looks at the door and greets us with a smile, except Mikayla, who starts to hum a familiar sounding tune.

"What is that?" Jess asks as she looks at her with a puzzled expression.

"It's the graduation song, duh," she replies.

"Congrats Tori! Are you excited to go home?" Liv asks me.

"Yes and no. It's complicated. I'm going to miss you guys though," I answer. "Well, hey, how about one last game of Uno Attack?" Andrew asks.

"You're on!" I say as I sit down with the rest of the group. As Mikayla shuffles and deals the cards out to everyone; I look around at everyone. Mike is next to me, being his usual cute self. Next to him Jess, looking much healthier these days than she did the first time I met her. Next to her is Liv, with arms that are healing up really nicely. Next to her is Andrew, actually smiling. That was a very rare thing to see for a while, but he actually looks and sounds happy now. Lastly is Mikayla, my first friend here. I can't imagine what my time here would've been like without her. Without her, I probably wouldn't have ever given any of these other people a chance, and I can't imagine what this experience would've been without these people I can now call true friends.

For some reason, people tend to romanticise mental illness. Being depressed or anxious or having a personality disorder or eating disorder has become this "beautiful" thing to people, and I'm not totally sure why. It's sad really, because it stigmatises mental illness, but the truth is, it is not something to be desired. People don't' realise that situational depression is not the same as clinical depression, and everyone who comes to St Vincent' Hospital, Ward C, is going through serious stuff. We didn't ask for this, and we definitely don't romanticise. This is our lives, all day, every day, not just something we use as a crutch to play the victim. I have so much respect for every single one of these people.

I jump a little when I hear the beep of the Uno Attack machine, and my thoughts are interrupted.

"You good?" Mike whispers to me. He can just always tell when my mind is in the clouds.

"Yeah, I'm good. I'm ready now," I say back to him with a smile. A true, genuine, smile, and it feels pretty damn good.

"Your turn, Tori," Liv says to me.

"Alright, let's do this," I say as I rub my hands together and get ready to press the Uno Attack button.

Ward C. C doesn't stand Crazy. C stands for Courageous. It stands for Can Do Anything. It stands for Capable. C doesn't stand for Crazy; it stands for Champion.

**Part Three
Future**

Chapter One
A Whole New Beginning

"Through happiness, I have smiled.
Through sadness, I have cried.
Through loss, I have coped.
Through adversity, I have overcome.
Through life, I have not lived.
Through it all, I have barely survived."

Geez, how I've missed writing in the public eye. It's been about three weeks since I've been home now, and sometimes I still forget that I don't have to hide my writing anymore. Dr S (she still hasn't told me her last name, by the way, but I'm okay with Dr. Sweetheart) has been pushing me to really focus on making sure that I acknowledge and appreciate the simple things in life that are so easy to take for granted, and on the top of that list is my love and talent for writing. As I'm just about to put my pen to paper again, my phone rings. I pick it up off my desk and it reads "Mikayla: FaceTime Call". That's another thing I won't take for granted: my phone. I definitely don't use or rely on it as much as I did, but still, balance is key. I answer it and instantly, Mikayla's face pops up on my phone, way too close to the screen.

"Heyyy girlllllllllll, what's up yo?" she says as she pulls the camera farther away from her face so I can actually see her.

"Hey Mikayla. What's going on?" I ask.

"I miss you, that's what's going on!" she replies, louder than I was expecting.

"I miss you too! How have you been feeling?" I ask. She left the hospital about a week or so after me, and as far as I know, she seems to be doing well.

"Good! I don't hear my voices as much, which is good, but sometimes, I feel lonely without them. Is that weird?" she asks.

"I mean... I guess not," I answer, not totally sure what to say. Everyone is entitled to their feelings, ya know, who am I to judge?

"I'm totally kidding, screw them. It feels awesome to have my own brain back. I love my medication. Does that make me sound like a druggie? I don't care, I'm saying it. I love my medication!"

"Why are you talking so fast?" I ask with a giggle.

"I'm just happy to talk to you, I miss my roomie!" she exclaims.

"I miss you too. We should hang out sometime soon."

"Oh my God, yes, I would love that! I have some new history jokes for you. Like this one! Who invented fractions?" she asks, knowing very well that I will probably not understand the joke anyway.

"Hmmm, I don't know. Who?" I reply in a lovingly sarcastic way.

218

"Henry the Fourth!" she answers followed by a hearty chuckle. Hers, of course, not mine. I just sit there in silence, as I'm sure she was already expecting.

"Fine. Not my best. I'll have a better one for you when I see you!" she exclaims with the utmost confidence.

"I'm sure you will. I probably won't get it, but I'm eager to hear it regardless," I say as she rolls her eyes back at me, also in a lovingly sarcastic way.

"So, any word from Jessica or Liv?" I ask. I left the hospital before anyone else, so I'm not really sure the status of their treatment plans.

"I actually spoke to Jess yesterday. She got out two days ago. She said that Andrew seems to be doing well, but you know, it's hard to tell with him since he's always so quiet. She also said that Liv was scheduled to leave the same day as her, but she had some kind of episode or something the night before. They extended her stay another week. Apparently, she tried to cut herself with a sharp piece of plastic she broke off of a fork," she says, and instantly, my heart drops. Ugh, poor thing.

"Damn, I hope she's okay," I respond. I love Jess, of course, like I love all of them, but I've always had a soft spot for Liv. We can relate to each other when it comes to the depression and the cutting. I feel bad for her, I wish there was something I could do to help. Relapses happen, but she's tough. I'm sure she'll bounce back, even stronger, and when she does, I'll be here for her. I know how it feels to have no one, I would never want her to feel that way. I've been able to fight off my urges with the help of Dr S., and Mike has been really supportive and attentive to helping me with relapsing tendencies and thoughts, but it's definitely not an easy task. I

219

look down at my recently cast-free arm and reflect on my own scars.

"I'll have to see her when she gets home," I say as I look back up at Mikayla.

"We should all hang out when everyone's home! I miss everyone," she says.

"That would be a nice reunion. I miss everyone too," I reply.

"Well, I'm sure you can't be missing Mike too much. When he left, he said the first thing he was going to do is call you. Did he, did he?" she asks, all excited, clearly fishing for some juicy details.

"He did, actually. We've been talking pretty much every day since he got home," I answer, trying to sound all cool and nonchalant about it, when really, I have butterflies going wild in my stomach just talking about it.

"Dude, that's awesome. Have you seen each other since the hospital?" she asks me.

"A couple of times. Dinners, movies, the usual stuff," I calmly answer her. "Dude. You guys are dating, and you didn't think to pick up the phone and call your best friend?" she asks. I didn't really ever think about it, but I guess Mikayla is my best friend. I haven't really had a true one since I was a child, I kind of forgot what it feels like.

"We're not exclusively dating. We're just casually hanging out," I say in defence.

"Oh please! You guys are so totally a thing. It's only a matter of time before things get labelled. And you better tell me this time, young lady!" she says, and I can tell she's serious.

"I promise," I say, as I hold my pinky up to the phone. She reciprocates, and the virtual pinky swear is in full affect.

"Mikayla, come on down for breakfast. And feed your damn guinea pigs!

They won't stop their squealing!" I hear from a distant voice.

"You have guinea pigs?" I ask. It's funny, Mikayla may be my best friend, but I realise now that I don't actually know all that much about her everyday life or world. Just all of the internal demons she faces and how her mind works. Normally, it's reversed. It's like a backwards way of starting a friendship. I wouldn't change it, though. She is my best friend, after all, and I do love her.

"Yeah, Amelia and Madison. Amelia Earhart and Dolley Madison." Typical Mikayla.

"I can't even say I'm surprised," I respond.

"You shouldn't be. Love you, bye!"

Before I could say anything else, she hangs up in a flash. It feels good to have a best friend again. I never thought that would happen again, but I'm glad it has. I put my phone back down on the desk and get back to writing.

"Through happiness, I have smiled.
Through sadness, I have cried.
Through loss, I have coped.
Through adversity, I have overcome.
Through life, I will continue to live.
Through it all, I will survive."

A best friend, a therapist I like, and dare I say, a maybe boyfriend? The possibility of recovery, help and hope? Who

221

would've ever thought? It's like a whole new beginning for me. I can't change the past and how my story began, but I can fight for an amazing ending, and I fully intend to continue to do so.

Chapter Two
The Book I'll Someday Write

Easy like Sunday morning. I know it sounds corny, but there's really nothing like the calmness of a warm and sunny Sunday morning in the heart of springtime. I really can never sleep in much anymore. I guess my body is still used to the St Vincent's time clock. I don't really mind, though. Lying in bed in the morning, watching the sun come up and relaxing has become my favourite part of the day. Sometimes I use that time to try and meditate and prepare myself mentally for the day. Two more things that I am learning to fully be aware of, taking in and appreciating: the nature around me, and my new morning routine. Dr S will be so proud.

One of the DBT (Dialectical Behaviour Therapy) skills that she's helped me implement since I left the hospital is the five senses technique. I use it sometimes to ground myself and keep me in the moment. Lying in bed, looking around my bedroom and out of the windows across from me, I start mentally taking note of all that's surrounds me.

Five things I can see:

1. The beautiful, fiery colours of the sunrise in the distance.
2. The birds eating from Dad's favourite bird feeder on the tree outside my window.
3. The keychain that Mike gave me on my last day at St Vincent's on my nightstand.
4. The pen and paper on my desk that I've been using daily since I got back home.
5. My handy-dandy popcorn ceiling above me.

Four things I can feel:

1. The comfort and softness of my mattress, comforter, sheets and favourite pillow.
2. The warmth of the just risen sun coming through my window.
3. The breeze from outside flowing into my room though the window that's cracked open.
4. The fur on the teddy bear that my aunt gave me when I was a kid that's sitting on the right side of the bed next to me.

Three things I can hear:

1. My phone's text tone going off to my left.
2. The same birds that I can see outside of my window chirping while they eat their breakfast.
3. The news from the television downstairs, just like I hear every other Sunday morning.

Two things I can smell:

1. My mom's world-famous homemade banana bread baking in the oven.
2. My dad's all familiar, never changing cologne (yes, it's that strong that I can smell it from all the way up here).

One thing I can taste:

1. …………

Okay, so the taste one can't always apply, but you get my point. Soon I'll be tasting my mom's world-famous homemade banana bread that I smell. That works.

Speaking of hearing my phone, I roll over to my left to pick it up off of my nightstand. Mike texted me, and instantly I feel my mouth curl into a smile before even reading it. I guess he doesn't sleep in much, either.

"Good morning, beautiful. I'll pick you up around 9:45 am for church. Can't wait to see you." My heart skipped a beat reading that text.

"Good morning. Can't wait. See you soon" I send back, followed by that smiling, blushing emoji. I put my phone down and let out a sigh. I feel so Zen right now; so calm, so content, like everything that's supposed to be happening is, and that's a feeling I've never had before.

As soon as I put my phone down, it goes off again. I pick it back up, but this time, it's from Dr S, reminding me to get my weekly task done before I see her again in two days. Another thing she and I have been working on is my self-worth and being kind to myself as I am to others. To treat myself the way I treat others and look at myself as equal rather than less than. This week's assignment: write a letter to my past self, being the person, I am now that I needed when I was younger when life started going downhill. It's interesting: the first letter she had me write to myself was a suicide note, and now this one is the complete opposite. I like this assignment; I definitely needed someone when I was younger to show me that they cared. Someone I could go to and lean on for support. Someone to care about me the way the Unsinkable Molly Brown cared about all those people she barely even knew. It's all moot now, but still, maybe things would have been different if I had just one person who cared. That's why I fight so hard to be that person for everyone; to show whoever needs it that I care about them, and that they are not alone.

I get up from my bed in my baggy sweatshirt and plaid pyjama pants and go over to my mirror. I reach over onto my dresser and grab the Aquaphor off of it. I begin to pull down my pants just a bit to expose my hip and thigh. I stare at the newest artwork permanently added to my body: a dreamcatcher. All of my tattoos mean something, and this one is no different from the rest. As a kid, I was always prone to general nightmares. As I got older, life went on, the world got harder, I went to St Vincent's and became prone to night terrors. As these obstacles of life took over, I lost my ability to dream, but not just when I slept. I lost a vision, a passion and any sense of hopes and dreams I've had for myself. Where I am right now, and with the help of Dr S., a spark has been ignited inside of me again. My lifelong dream has always been to be an author, but always seemed so farfetched.

For the first time, I feel it's even slightly possible. Not only has that lifelong dream been recognised again, but I also discovered another dream: to help people, save lives, and change the world. I'm hoping one day my books can assist me with that, and that both of those dreams will work together. My new dreamcatcher tattoo will ensure that I will keep those dreams close to my mind and my heart, and remind me of that desire to dream and that motivation to fulfil them in the tough moments of life when I start to forget.

I pull my pants back up and head over to my desk. As I do every time I'm about to sit down and write something of importance that requires complete concentration and focus, I put on my salt lamp and light my candle. This week's pick is Bath & Body Works Vanilla & Peach Tea. I set the aura, pick up my pen, and get to work.

Dear You,

I know how you feel. Lonely, broken, worthless. Like you wish you were never born. Because what's the point of existing in a world like this when you're living a life like this? You feel like anything, even death, has to be better than this. Like no one would care if you were gone, and some wouldn't even notice. You're more afraid to live than you are to die. Believe it or not, I do know how you feel. I was you: I was in your exact same shoes once. Listen to me when I tell you that even though you feel completely insignificant, you matter. God chose you, and while this may be hard for you to understand right now, that makes you very significant, and very special.

When those kids bully you, it's because of their own insecurities. And when those teachers witness you being

227

bullied and pretend they don't, it's because of their own demons. You feel that the cruelness of the world and the sins from these people have defined you. While this has all impacted the woman you are, they do not define you. Not even your own self-inflicted scars have to define you, and it's okay, I know there's a lot of them. I know how deep your self-loathing goes, and I know how worthless you feel on this Earth, but let me tell you, you are stronger than you could ever possibly imagine.

I know how hard it is to feel strong and like you can overcome anything that comes your way. While you don't always think you can, I promise you, you can, and you will. I know how hard it is to try and find reasons to go on in life, and I know how easy it is to feel like the whole world's against you and that things will never get better. The truth is, life isn't always fair, and there isn't anything you can do to change that. I'll be honest with you; it's going to get worse before it gets better. Life is going to throw obstacles and struggles your way, and sometimes, you are going to give in. You are going to feel like you can't go on, and you are going to deal with that feeling in some pretty self-destructive ways.

Again, I was you, I know that that stuff is going to happen, but I also know that you are going to come out on the other side like the warrior you are. When you are in it, nothing else matters, but once you're on the outside of it, you see the truth, and the truth is, you got this. You will hit rock bottom and feel lower than you ever thought you possibly could. You are going to be in so much pain that it physically hurts you and you can't understand how your heart is still beating through the pain. I also know that you will come through it like a champion. That lowest point, that rock bottom, that is going *to be exactly what turns your life around. Once you hit that, you are going to be forced into the reality that is survival, and you are going to find your motivation and drive to work your ass off to get yourself better. Along the way, things will happen that you never thought would. You'll make friends, you'll find someone you like talking to that actually helps you, and you'll even move on from what that boy did to you. Your heart will be able to love again, and you will be able to feel loved again too. You are in a place right now where you can't even begin to see what's on the other side after you overcome all of this heartache, but I see it. I am living it, and I can't wait for that part of your life to begin. You can't change the past, but you can fight like hell to impact your future, and trust me, you will.*

Robin Williams once said: "No matter what people tell you, words and ideas can change the world." Writing has saved me so many times from the darkest depths of my urges to destructive patterns. I know how powerful words can be. I have a story to tell, and lives to save, starting with yours. Someday, I am going to write that book, not just for you, but for every person who feels the same way I did and the same way you do right now. I promise you. Never give up. Trust me.

Always,
Me